BLONDE ON THE SPOT

THE CLASSIC HANK JANSON

The first original Hank Janson book appeared in 1946, and the last in 1971. However, the classic era on which we are focusing in the Telos reissue series lasted from 1946 to 1953. The following is a checklist of those books, which were subdivided into five main series and a number of 'specials'.

PRE-SERIES BOOKS
When Dames Get Tough (1946)
Scarred Faces (1947)

SERIES ONE
1) This Woman Is Death (1948)
2) Lady, Mind That Corpse (1948)
3) Gun Moll For Hire (1948)
4) No Regrets For Clara (194)
5) Smart Girls Don't Talk (1949)
6) Lilies For My Lovely (1949)
7) Blonde On The Spot (1949)
8) Honey, Take My Gun (1949)
9) Sweetheart, Here's Your Grave (1949)
10) Gunsmoke In Her Eyes (1949)
11) Angel, Shoot To Kill (1949)
12) Slay-Ride For Cutie (1949)

SERIES TWO
13) Sister, Don't Hate Me (1949)
14) Some Look Better Dead (1950)
15) Sweetie, Hold Me Tight (1950)
16) Torment For Trixie (1950)
17) Don't Dare Me, Sugar (1950)
18) The Lady Has A Scar (1950)
19) The Jane With The Green Eyes (1950)
20) Lola Brought Her Wreath (1950)
21) Lady, Toll The Bell (1950)
22) The Bride Wore Weeds (1950)
23) Don't Mourn Me Toots (1951)
24) This Dame Dies Soon (1951)

SERIES THREE
25) Baby, Don't Dare Squeal (1951)
26) Death Wore A Petticoat (1951)
27) Hotsy, You'll Be Chilled (1951)

28) It's Always Eve That Weeps (1951)

29) Frails Can Be So Tough (1951)
30) Milady Took The Rap (1951)
31) Women Hate Till Death (1951)
32) Broads Don't Scare Easy (1951)
33) Skirts Bring Me Sorrow (1951)
34) Sadie Don't Cry Now (1952)
35) The Filly Wore A Rod (1952)
36) Kill Her If You Can (1952)

SERIES FOUR
37) Murder (1952)
38) Conflict (1952)
39) Tension (1952)
40) Whiplash (1952)
41) Accused (1952)
42) Killer (1952)
43) Suspense (1952)
44) Pursuit (1953)
45) Vengeance (1953)
46) Torment (1953)
47) Amok (1953)
48) Corruption (1953)

SERIES 5
49) Silken Menace (1953)
50) Nyloned Avenger (1953)

SPECIALS
Auctioned (1952)
Persian Pride (1952)
Desert Fury (1953)
One Man In His Time (1953)
Unseen Assassin (1953)
Deadly Mission (1953)

BLONDE ON THE SPOT

HANK JANSON

First published in United Kingdom in 2005 by
Telos Publishing Ltd
17 Pendre Avenue, Prestatyn, LL19 9SH
www.telos.co.uk

Telos Publishing Ltd values feedback. Please e-mail us with
any comments you may have about this book to:
feedback@telos.co.uk

This edition © 2013 Telos Publishing Ltd

ISBN: 978-1-84583-875-1

Introduction © 2005 Steve Holland
Novel by Stephen D Frances
Cover by Reginald Heade
With thanks to Steve Holland
www.hankjanson.co.uk

The Hank Janson name, logo and silhouette device are
registered trademarks of Telos Publishing Ltd

First published in England by S D Frances, June 1949

British Library Cataloguing in Publication Data.
A catalogue record for this book is available from the British
Library.

PUBLISHER'S NOTE

The appeal of the Hank Janson books to a modern readership lies not only in the quality of the storytelling, which is as powerfully compelling today as it was when they were first published, but also in the fascinating insight they afford into the attitudes, customs and morals of the 1940s and 1950s. We have therefore endeavoured to make *Blonde on the Spot*, and all our other Hank Janson reissues, as faithful to the original editions as possible. Unlike some other publishers, who when reissuing vintage fiction have been known edit it to remove aspects that might offend present-day sensibilities, we have left the original narrative absolutely intact.

The original editions of these classic Hank Janson titles made quite frequent use of phonetic 'Americanisms' such as 'kinda', 'gotta', 'wanna' and so on. Again, we have left these unchanged in the Telos Publishing Ltd reissues, to give readers as genuine as possible a taste of what it was like to read these books when they first came out, even though such devices have since become sorta out of fashion.

The only amendments we have made to the

original text have been to correct obvious lapses in spelling, grammar and punctuation – for instance, inserting question marks at the ends of questions in the many places where they were mistakenly omitted – and to remedy clear typesetting errors and inconsistencies – such as where the place called Ghost City was sometimes referred to instead as Ghost Town (in fact, the two names were used almost interchangeably in parts of the original, but we have chosen to standardise on the former).

Lastly, we should mention that we have made every effort to trace and acquire relevant copyrights in the various elements that make up this book. However, if anyone has any further information that they could provide in this regard, we would be very grateful to receive it.

INTRODUCTION

Continuity played an important part in the Hank Janson saga. For the bulk of Hank's adventures, he was a crime reporter with the *Chicago Chronicle*. Welcoming back fellow workers like his cigar-chomping boss, Chief Healey, and following his on-off romance with woman's page editor, Sheila Lang, were fun aspects of the stories.

There are two particularly fine examples of this continuity. One occurs in *Vengeance*, where Hank visits a location he has previously written about in *It's Always Eve That Weeps* (a novel that does not feature Hank as a character); the second is the ongoing storyline between *Lilies For My Lovely* and *Blonde On The Spot*.

What makes this such an interesting follow-up is not simply the continuity of characters – it was neither the first nor the last time that a character would be with Hank at the end of one book and still be there at the beginning of the next. The real interest lies in how Hank's relationship with his *amour* has developed between the two stories.

Sally Taylor is the main focus of Hank's attentions in *Lilies For My Lovely*. The two meet in Des Moines, where Sally is living for a few months with her uncle.

Hank spies a pretty dame and – being an inveterate stalker of women – decides to follow her. When this attractive girl gets her heel caught in a grille in the sidewalk, he is on hand to help, which he does with all the usual Janson (lack of) finesse. Hank gets an eyeful of her legs (there are soft dimples in the backs of her knees) and her foot (dainty, beautifully formed), but manages to leave the heel behind when he wrenches her shoe out of the grate.

Over the length of the day, Hank and Sally enjoy each other's company, wisecracking with each other, having a flutter on the horses, going swimming, and generally having a whale of a time. Hank is shocked to hear the next day that Sally has died of heart failure – but he quickly convinces himself that no girl so full of vital, vibrant life and animal strength could die so suddenly.

As the plot of *Lilies* unfolds, Hank is proved to be right: Sally's 'death' is part of a kidnapping plot by her uncle and a rogue named Dr Spiller. Hank eventually catches up with them in Sally's home town, Mason City, where he discovers Sally tied up in the basement of her house along with the kidnapped girl, June Miller. Sally is threatened with death by various ghastly methods, and eventually Hank rescues her from a hole dug in the basement, where she is buried up to the neck in quick-drying cement.

Sally survives this horrific ordeal with surprisingly little psychological damage, and she and Hank enjoy a happy relationship. As *Lilies For My Lovely* comes to an end, they have been together for around nine weeks and are heading off in Hank's car toward what should be a bright future.

How wrong could Hank be? Three months later, as

Blonde On The Spot opens, Hank tells his readers:
'Beneath the outward veneer of fun and excitement,
there was a strain of awkwardness.' What he once saw as
'a real pleasant smile' has turned into a stubborn frown;
Sally's fascinating, animal litheness has lost its allure; the
wisecracking banter has dried up. Small things begin to
annoy Hank, building up a tension between the two
until he snaps and Sally responds with stony silence.

This is the situation in which Hank finds himself in
the opening chapters of *Blonde*, the seventh full-length
Hank Janson novel. On its origin publication, in June
1949, the cover, the most provocative so far, boasted
'250,000 sale' and showed a young blonde girl in a
ragged blue dress tied to a chair.[1] The dress is barely able
to contain her bosom. Readers waiting for the book to
live up to the promise of the cover would not be
disappointed – Hank eventually ropes up three girls,
although none in quite the manner that cover artist
Reginald 'Heade' Webb depicted.

The blonde – Blondie – is one of the subsidiary
participants in a story that rather overflows with
characters. Indeed, the book is possibly too chock-full of
people and incidents for its own good. Author Stephen
Frances was obviously growing more comfortable
wearing the shoes of his lead character, although he still
seems to have had a few problems squaring incidents
that he wanted to appear in the story and relating how
Hank should react to them. There was the frequent
problem in the Hank Janson novels of violence against
women. To give his readers the vicarious thrills that they

---

[1] A 1953 reissue used a slightly revised cover with the sale figure now
8,000,000 and the price raised from 1/6 to 2/-.

were demanding, Hank had to be thrown into situations with young women whose morality was suspect. What better way to get Hank hot under the collar than to have him mixed up in a rough and tumble with three prostitutes? After all, it was their job to wear the kind of clothes that would arouse Hank and his readers and not feel embarrassed when they were somehow removed or torn off.

But this was a series of novels available to anybody walking into a newsagent's, and sex as a subject matter was not only frowned upon by the authorities but also actively discouraged through prosecution of said newsagents, as well as of publishers and even, in extreme cases, of authors. *Lady Chatterley's Lover* was available to only a tiny readership in the UK at that time, and then only when rare copies escaped the attention of customs officers. The authorized British edition published by Martin Secker in 1932 was heavily bowdlerized; Heinemann's 1956 edition followed the same text. It was as late as 1960 before Penguin Books finally took a stand and published the unexpurgated text, prepared to defend the artistic merit of a book they knew would be prosecuted under the Obscene Publications Act.

This act of defiance was possible only thanks to Hank Janson, whose publisher and distributor were successfully prosecuted in 1954 over the publication of seven novels deemed to be obscene. The fall-out from the trial – in which a variety of other books were introduced by the defence to try to establish what was easily available and acceptable to modern readers – led to a change in the law, allowing artistic merit to be taken into consideration when judging novels that dealt with sex in a more candid way than some would like.[2]

To give the readers what they wanted and keep himself out of prison, author Frances trod a very fine line with sex and violence. Writing in 1949, two years before the first major prosecution of a paperback publisher, Frances had already drawn a line for himself – and occasionally strayed over it. Hank would often state that he did not believe in violence towards women. He gives perhaps his definitive statement on this during a tussle with Elsa Crane in *Honey, Take My Gun*: 'If she'd been a fella, I could have got in under her guard and lifted her clean off the ground with an uppercut. But you don't treat dames that way – at least, I don't.' Yet in Chapter Ten of the book you are now holding, he has a slightly different attitude:

> I suddenly realised that I was nearly a goner. They had only to get my legs roped and I'd be a plaything for them to handle. If I didn't get loose from this quickly …
>
> I saw it differently then. They were dames, and subconsciously I'd been treating them like dames. If I was gonna get out of this, I was gonna have to forget they were dames!
>
> I forgot they were dames! Somehow I managed to twist my head and open my mouth. And then I bit. I bit as hard as I knew how. I didn't know or care what part of

---

[2] The full story of the various legal trials faced by the Hank Janson novels can be found in *The Trials Of Hank Janson* by Steve Holland (London, Telos Publishing, 2004).

Helga it was that I bit, provided I got free.
Jezus, what a howl that girl gave. She leaped up so suddenly, she almost took my teeth with her. That left my shoulders loose so I could strain upwards and clop Blondie under the chin.

Hank squares this violence with himself by the simple justification that if he doesn't do something, he's going to get hurt. A human reaction, but hardly an ethical one, given his moral stance. Almost certainly, author Frances was trusting that his readers would remember that Hank is fighting with three prostitutes who have left their own morals behind and given up any rights to be treated like women.

Violence toward women is not the only problem with *Blonde On The Spot*. In a book full of clichéd characters, the worst treatment is reserved for members of a Native American tribe. The setting for the book is Oklahoma City and a nearby ghost town called Ghost City. No doubt Frances was inspired by this setting to create a plot based around a conflict between cowboys and Indians. The local reservation is owned by the Choctaw tribe, originally based in central Mississippi when they met their first Europeans in the 16th Century. The leaders of the tribe signed a treaty in 1820 ceding their lands in exchange for land in Oklahoma. Many of the tribesmen refused to move West voluntarily. Most were forced to walk to their new land along what became known as the Trail of Tears in the bitter winter of 1831-32. A quarter of those who started out died from exposure and cholera on the trip, and the new land was not ready for the survivors when they arrived: food and medicine were short and a flood the following spring destroyed many of the crops they planted.

Over 100 years later – the novel is set in modern (1949) Oklahoma – the Choctaw Indians as depicted by Frances are straight out of a B-movie. 'Want'um squaw,' growls one whiskey-fuelled redskin on the warpath, in pidgin English that would shame Tonto. 'You give, then go. No kill.'

In movie terms, the idea of a modern-day battle between cowboys and Indians would be called a set piece. Imagine what it would be like with Indians with bows and arrows and tomahawks attacking a car instead of a stagecoach. Whilst it may have sounded good when Frances pitched the idea to himself, the end results are embarrassingly bad. Jimmy Chark, part-Indian, is depicted as stoic and brave; but every other mention of Indians reverts to that peculiar Wild West of Hollywood.

The cover of the '12th Reprint' reissue. Advertised on the back of this edition was the planned fifth series book 'Perfumed Nemesis', which in the event was never published.

The chiefs of the tribal reservations swap furs for whiskey and, once they are fired up with white man's firewater, the whole sorry mess degenerates into scenes of painted braves performing dances to the frenzied beat of tom-toms and riding into town to scalp'um white men.

Not that *Blonde On The Spot* doesn't have its good points. As mentioned above, Frances was growing more comfortable with the character he had created, and finding his voice as a writer. Hank's background was being slowly sketched in: in *Lilies*, we get a hint that Hank has been a newspaperman when he says (of some photos): 'Tell her that you know a fella that'd like to give these to his editor.' In *Blonde*, the reference is more specific: 'I began to tell her about myself, the things I'd done, the places I'd been to and how I was working my way leisurely across the States with money to burn in my pockets.' When his friend Victor introduces Hank to a young reporter, it is as 'a real reporter': 'He's covered some of the toughest assignments New York can dish out.'

The first trip Hank makes to Ghost City results in him playing the roulette wheel using a system that was developed by Frances's friend Harry Whitby. The system – described in Whitby's *Science Of Gambling*, which Frances had published in 1945 – worked only on a crooked table and relied on playing 'corpse' by backing small amounts of money against the play of bets, trusting the house to fix it so it would fleece the greater amounts. Frances had already described this system in his earlier, non-Janson novel *One Man In His Time*, and would later do so again in *Frails Can Be So Tough* (another Janson title available in Telos's reissue series).

Blonde on the Spot is also laced with the kind of sly,

innuendo-filled humour that Hank's readers appreciated:

> She said: 'You've got pretty big teeth, aincher?'
> The car lurched, pressing us all over to one side. Helga was pressed against me like we were glued together.
> 'Yeah, and you've got pretty big ...' I began, and then suddenly remembered that Sally was in front. She might not have liked the kinda crack I was gonna make.

The novel's ending, with its Indian uprising, the destruction of Ghost City and the murder and/or scalping of many white folks, makes barely a ripple with the police, but realism isn't always the point of a Hank Janson novel. Janson fans would have been far more concerned with Hank's dilemma of how to get three barely-dressed dames into a flat without arousing suspicions. Typically, the solution involves getting a fourth dame out of her dress.

It might not be Pulitzer Prize-winning literature, but it sure helped shift copies off the shelves.

Steve Holland,
Colchester, July 2005

1

It's about five hundred miles from Des Moines to Oklahoma City, and you can drive the whole distance in twenty-four hours if you're crazy to get there in a hurry.

Me and Sally weren't in a hurry. We took our time on the way, stopping at hotels when it suited us, sometimes camping, using the camping equipment I carried in the car, and sometimes stopping at roadhouses, sleeping in wooden chalets and walking and exploring the country by day.

All told, it took us three months to make the trip from Des Moines to Oklahoma, and the way we travelled took us through Missouri, Nebraska and Kansas.

Travelling those wide, macadam roads, passing through city after city, each with its quota of towering skyscrapers, its busy, bustling offices and factories, I found it hard to believe that just a short seventy years earlier, Billy the Kid was riding the trail through this same country; that roaming Indian tribes lay in wait for unwary caravans; and that thousands of head of cattle were herded across dusty plains.

The West is young, yet it is rich in its short history.

Men have built cities from grasslands in the short span of a lifetime and fed those cities by rail, road and air. Those cities are as modern and as thriving as some cities in other parts of the world that have taken ten and more generations to grow to maturity.

The men who first helped to build the West had vision and foresight, and their children have benefited. Travelling through Kansas, we passed some of the most wonderful farming country it is possible to even dream about. Folk in Kansas told us with a smile that they had grasshoppers as big as mules. Farmers told us they had farms so large that by the time the mortgage was concluded on the West side, the East side had become due. The folk there tell a folk story about a guy named Lem Blanchard. He climbed a stalk of grass one day. After he'd looked into the next county, he found the stalk was growing upwards faster than he could clamber down. He was finally shot by his neighbours as an act of kindness to save him from slow death by starvation. Others told us that the land is so fertile that when you sow a seed, you first poke a hole in the ground, then drop the seed in and step back quickly to avoid having your head knocked off.

Yeah, Kansas is a rich, plentiful country, and some day, when I've made my pile, I'm gonna settle somewhere in Kansas.

We crossed the border between Kansas and Oklahoma, riding a high, wide road lined with telegraph poles and electricity pylons. There was a lotta traffic on the road, huge trucks, fast cars and long distance coaches. When we shot across the border, a coupla speed cops gave us a disinterested glance.

Seventy years ago, men would have reined in at this spot, circled the surrounding country with a watchful eye, beat the dust from their clothes and fumbled for a bag of shag. Behind, in front and around them would have stretched open country with never a sign of human existence to be seen.

It's pretty certain that those forefathers of ours would have been watchful at this spot. Maybe one of them would have spat tobacco juice on the dry ground, loosened his colt and said quietly: 'This y'ere's Injun country.'

Maybe that's true today, still. It's reckoned that more than a third of all the Indians in the whole United States are resident in Oklahoma,

They don't wear feathered headdresses and blankets any longer. They've abandoned their ponies for the tramcar and their blankets for lounge suits. In fact, the Indian has become as much part of the American people as have the Irish, the Dutch, the English and the French. They are American citizens now, with full rights of citizenship, many of them having risen to prominence and occupying positions of great distinction in all professions as well as in politics.

There's a story that I heard in Oklahoma that's reputed to be true. It concerns that famous American humorist Will Rogers and shows how much the Indian has become assimilated by the American nation. Will Rogers was in conversation with a New England lady who asked him if his people had come over to America on the Mayflower. Will Rogers tousled his hair, grinned and said: 'No, ma'am, but we met the boat.'

But there are still a number of Indians who have refused to accept the pressure of civilisation. These are the reservation Indians, the blanket Indians as they are called. They live in reservations, are untaxed and live the way of life they wish to live, in huts or tepees, cut off from the amenities of civilisation but protected by the law from crafty businessmen who otherwise would cheat them of their birthright.

Me and Sally wisecracked as we drove along. That's the way it was with us all the time, wisecracking, laughing and enjoying each other's company.

But beneath the outward veneer of fun and excitement there was growing a strain of awkwardness. It wasn't that we didn't get along well together. It was just that ... well ... it just does happen that way sometimes. You meet a dame, you like her and she likes you. Then for a time everything is wonderful and you wouldn't ever want things to be any different.

Then, after a time, a little thing she does gets you on the raw. Maybe she's done it hundreds of times before but you haven't noticed it previously. You've noticed it only the last dozen or so times. And after that, it gets worse and worse. Because now you begin to look for it, you begin to wait for it to happen, and all the time your nerves are getting all set to screech when it does happen.

And all that happens over a little thing that you wouldn't think about twice, normally.

Sally had one or two little habits like that – poking me with her forefinger was one of them. Whenever she wanted to attract my attention, or maybe when she was about to say something that she thought I oughta give all my attention to, she'd jab me with her forefinger: 'Oh, Hank,' she'd say.

That forefinger began to loom large in my world. It got so that most of the day I was tensed, waiting for that forefinger to jab me. It didn't hurt me a little bit. But it got me so tensed, I'd have rather had a poke in the puss with a knuckle-duster than a gentle jab with that forefinger.

I'd begun keeping count, and the day we rolled into Oklahoma City, I'd been fore fingered exactly eleven times since breakfast.

There was another thing she did, too, that got me mad. She sometimes wore a pearl necklace. And when she wore it, she'd suck the necklace and try to talk through it.

She got me so mad doing this, I bawled her out on it. That got her mad then, and she went into a sulk that lasted several hours. Now, like most men, sulking is something that drives me crazy. If I do something that gets a dame sore, I'm ready to apologise if I'm in the wrong, and I'm even ready to apologise if I'm in the right – provided it makes the dame happy and she knows that I meant what I said when I bawled her out.

But this sulking business … whew! Every time I saw I her scowling puss staring stony-faced, dead straight ahead of her, it got me so mad I wanted to draw into the side of the road and shove her out on her fanny.

'Okay,' I thought. 'What's the point in making I ourselves unhappy? Let's enjoy life.' So I leaned over and said in a friendly way: 'Snap out of it, honey. Let's go some place and enjoy ourselves.'

No reply. Stony silence.

'Where'd ya like to go, honey? '

More silence. Only this was a painful silence. It kinda sat all round me like a wall of ice. It got me annoyed.

'Look,' I said, 'If you don't want me around, you can get out and walk.'

'I don't care,' she said. Her voice was emotionless.

I twisted the wheel savagely, swerved into the side of the road and pulled up with a squeal of brakes.

'Okay,' I yelled. 'Start walking.'

She sat there like a stone image. I waited. Then I lit I a cigarette and worked my way through it. The wall of ice was still surrounding me. Sally just sat staring in front of her. She didn't make any move to get outta the car. But she didn't get friendly either.

After I'd reached the end of the cigarette I heaved a sigh of exasperation.

'You getting out? '

'I'll get out at the next town,' she said.

I breathed a loud, deep sigh of disgust, let up the clutch and drove on.

When we got to the next town, I drove right through it until I got to the outskirts at the far end, and then I said: 'Look, honey. There's no future in us being this way. How's about us being friendly?'

Stony silence.

I grunted, and for the second time slewed the wheel and braked abruptly at the side of the road.

'Okay,' I said. 'You're in a town now. You can start walking.'

Her face was quite composed as she turned in her seat and grabbed one of her small cases that was in the back. 'I shan't want the other stuff,' she said.

I looked at the case. It contained her nightwear and a few articles of toilet.

She got one hand on the door handle, pressed it down and opened the door. In another few seconds, she'd have been out on the sidewalk hot-footing for an hotel and a shakedown for the night. She couldn't have had much dough in her bag, and everything else she had in the whole wide world was in the rest of her cases stacked away in the back of my car.

Yet she wasn't hesitating. She'd have got out and

walked away from me just the way she was, little dough and no clothes apart from those she stood up in.

And why was she gonna do this?

She was gonna do it all on account I'd bawled her out for sucking her pearls.

That's the crazy kinda things dames do.

I reached over the front of her, grabbed the door just as it began to open, and slammed it shut again. Sally made a sudden movement like she was gonna try and get outta the car in a hurry. I let up the clutch (the engine was still running) and swung out on to the crown of the road. By the time she'd got the door open, I was doing twenty, and by the time she'd decided she would risk jumping out of the car at twenty miles an hour, I was doing forty. She slammed the door shut, glared at me and said:

'Stop and put me down, *if* you please.'

I went on driving.

She stamped her foot. 'Let me out,' she demanded.

'Shuddup,' I told her.

She sat there, fuming. There were wicked, angry flickers in her eyes, and I expected smoke to come out of her mouth at any moment.

'I demand to be put down,' she said.

'You're good and mad, aincher?'

'I am,' she said hotly.

'Thank God,' I said piously. 'For hours, you been sitting there like an obelisk. It's good to know you've got emotions, even if it is just sheer bad temper.'

She said something that sounded like 'Pswshaw' and relapsed into a sulk once again.

I drove for a solid three hours after that, trying to get her sociable the whole time. She was mildly non-committal at the end of those three hours, just enough to warrant stopping for something to eat. Fortunately the joint we stopped at sold hard liquor. I ordered a coupla ryes before we ate, and kept ordering them right through the meal. We both got warmed up a bit, and after we'd danced a bit, with the jukebox supplying the rhythm, we got sociable again.

But that sulking business didn't happen just once. It happened a great many times in the three months it took us to travel to Oklahoma City. That's what I mean when I say there was a glowing strain of awkwardness beneath the pleasant outer surface of our relationship.

And it probably wasn't all Sally's fault. I guess I ain't no better than the next fella. I mayn't have been too easy to get along with myself.

And that's the way things were going when we hit Oklahoma City at eleven o'clock one morning. And because things were that way, getting to Oklahoma City more or less decided the future issues for us.

Oklahoma City wasn't a bit like you'd imagine it to be if you'd been just a reader of Westerns. There were no hitching rails, sideboards, rangy cowhands or pony express stations.

Oklahoma City is as modern and more modern than New York. There's skyscrapers there, wide macadam roads, and the sidewalks are jammed with jostling clerks, businessmen and fashionably dressed women.

There's wealth in that town, too. The town itself literally floats on wealth. Oil, the liquid gold of the West, flows beneath the concrete foundations of thosa towering skyscrapers. Oil-filled derricks can be seen everywhere and there's even a derrick erected in the Governor's own private grounds.

And these derricks sometimes spring up overnight,

There's a reason for that. Oil ain't like coal. If some fella strikes coal or gold, it don't run away. It waits right there for him to come back with a pick and shovel and get right down to digging it out.

But oil's different. If you find oil, you gotta start pumping it up into your own pail right away. If you don't some fella is gonna dig a hole of his own maybe a hundred yards away. And as soon as he begins to pump, the oil at the bottom of your boring is gonna run straight over to his boring. Yeah, if you're ever lucky enough to strike oil, don't waste time. Just get down to pumping it up before some other guy starts in doing the same thing.

Me and Sally drove around the town for a time. Then we chose a quiet hotel, parked the car and washed, ready for lunch.

After lunch, we took coffee in the lounge with a Grand Marnier liqueur to round off the meal and sat reading the midday papers while we smoked. There was a tall, sun-burned, grey-haired man sitting opposite. Once or twice I'd seen him glancing towards us, and after a time he and asked for a light. He was smoking a small, brown cheroot. When he spoke, it was with a pronounced Southern drawl.

'Strangers hyar?' he asked conversationally.

'Just got in this morning,' I told him. Sally glanced up from reading the funnies, flicked her eyes across his face and then looked back at the paper again. In that short, single glance, she'd examined him, weighed him in the balance and discarded him as being dull and uninteresting.

'Ah kin tell from the way youse speak that youse from the North,' he said.

I felt like saying that I could tell from the way he spoke that he was from the South. But that may have seemed a little rude. I grinned and said: 'Sure, fella, I've had the bowery twang ever since the Dead End Kids hit the screen.'

He hadn't a sense of humour. He didn't know what to make of that. So he swallowed hard, cleared his throat and said: 'Mebbe youse would appreciate a li'lle advice about the parts hereabout?'

I began to tumble to his line then. Inevitably, in any town, there's sure to be a show of some kind going on. These shows aren't always strictly legal. And they bore the local citizens stiff. So there have to be fellas going around who whip up the sightseers. And sightseers were usually folks new to the town. This fella was doing his job, whipping up enthusiasm for some kinda racket.

But I'm a sucker for rackets. I like to see everything, and I like to see it for myself. It's caused by an irrepressible streak of curiosity that I've got. Many times, that streak of curiosity has got me in trouble. But I never learn.

I said mildly: 'Okay, fella, shoot. What's your racket?'

That took the wind outta his sails. He spluttered and managed to say: 'Racket, sir? Ahm afraid youse misjudging mah motives.'

'I ain't,' I told him. 'Don't lose your pants. I'm a customer. But give it to me short and sweet. Don't try leading me by the nose.'

'Ah confess, Ah doan't know what youse mean.'

'Can it,' I said. 'What's the play? Where is it? How much does it cost?'

He stared at me for a long time, his deep-set eyes reflecting his uncertainty. Probably he was upset at not being able to exercise his Southern charm and persuasion on me. Finally he said: 'Arh yuh a sporting gennelman?'

'That's me,' I said. 'I've been interested in sport ever since I was born. Harry the Horse useta be one of my best friends.'

His eyes shone. 'Ah mean real sport,' he said.

'Such as?' I probed.

'The wheel,' he said.

I tossed that around in my mind. He was talking about roulette. And that's a game that's always interested me. It's always interested me ever since the Greek Syndicate got to work at Monte Carlo and broke the bank three times.

He musta seen the interest in my eyes.

'It's on the level,' he said; and speaking without thinking like he was, the Southern drawl was partly lost and replaced by the clipped accent of a Northerner.

'Where do I go? '

He said: 'We dress it up a bit. Give the sightseers a spot of atmosphere. We give it the old Western touch.'

'I can imagine,' I said dryly. 'Where do I go?'

He pulled out a gold pencil and a card bearing his name. He wrote full and precise instructions on the card, telling me how to get there.

I tucked the card away in my breast pocket. 'Is this thing on the level for sure?' I asked.

'Of course,' he said. 'On muh word as a Southern gennelman.'

I hadn't believed him before. I certainly didn't believe him when he gave me that assurance.

But it didn't make any difference to me. I'm a sucker … within limits.

2

To start with, Sally didn't want to go. That gave a nice set-up to the evening, before we even left the hotel. She claimed she was tired and, after dinner, when I suggested we got going, she pouted and said she'd been looking forward to a quiet evening, reading, and then getting up to bed early.

I said that was fine. She could read and go to bed and I'd go out visiting.

Sally said she wasn't gonna be left alone in a strange hotel the first night in town.

I said that was fine. She could go get her coat and come with me.

That was when Sally began to sulk. She came with me, but she sulked all the time. It got me so mad, I began to wish like hell she wasn't coming with me.

But she got her coat and climbed into the car like she was going to an execution. I shot a quick glance at hard, emotionless face and swore softly to myself. It's one thing having a happy, carefree dame sitting on seat beside you and ready for any kinda excitement that might crop up, but it's entirely different to have a dame with you that's thoroughly miserable and determined to go on being miserable. That's the way dames get, though. They're all alike. You can be happy for a while, and then suddenly they wanna get good and miserable just for the hell of it. There's a poet fella who useta run around dashing off love poems. He knew a thing or two about dames. He oughta have done. According to history, he climbed in between the sheets with quite a number. But he summed up broads in a few nifty words. He said something like this: 'Women are impossible to live with ... or without!' The fella who wrote this was a Lord, an English Lord. His name was Byron. And I reckon he showed good, sound horse-sense.

So I drove off into the night, away from the city limit, with a bundle of misery perched on the seat beside me and wishing like hell I coulda left it behind to curl up in bed at the hotel.

Now don't get me wrong about Sally. I liked Sally. I liked her well. In fact, she was ace-high as far as I was concerned. But this sulking business was doing things. It was running my nerves ragged. It was getting me so I didn't even want her around when she was moody this way.

I drove on into the night, not saying a word, but all the time terribly conscious that she was sitting there, a kinda unpleasant burden that I had to carry around with me.

The imitation Southerner had given me pretty clear instructions. Apparently there was a ghost town about twenty miles outside of Oklahoma City. Fifty or sixty years earlier it had been the site of an oil well. Overnight it had become a small town, crammed with prospectors and miners. Oil had been struck and there was a rush to soak up the wealth.

First came the miners and the workers. Then came

the lawyers. Sturdy wooden buildings replaced the miners' tents. Then came the saloon bars with raw spirits, and finally the gamblers with their cards and wheels of chance.

That had lasted a coupla years, and then unexpectedly the oil well had petered out. Overnight the town had become deprived of its source of wealth. The miners had drifted away, the lawyers had had no clients they could tie in a knot, the gamblers had had nobody to fleece, and the saloon keepers had had nobody to sell hooch to. Within a month, the town had become deserted. Nobody bothered to pull down the town. Why should they? The whole town was left standing the way it was, empty, untended and silent. A ghost town! With only the whispering echoes of the voices from a bygone age to give it silent life.

That ghost town had stayed that way for two generations. Maybe a lonely coyote had howled through the silent streets. Perhaps a lonely cowhand, crossing the range, had unrolled his blanket for the night in the shelter of the gaming hall. But otherwise, the ghost town had been left alone to time and silence. And time had taken its toll. Bright paint peeled beneath the burning sun, the weather ate into the wood, hinges came adrift and windows fell askew, rotting beams gave beneath the weight of the roof, and fierce winds drifted sandy soil into the town so that it became half-submerged, partly buried in a sea of sand.

And it stayed that way until some smart fella realised the allure that a ghost town could exercise on a generation that had grown up in a world of concrete, cars and canned food.

He'd acquired rights to the ghost town. He'd spent good dough renovating the dump. As far as possible, it had been left just as it had been all those years earlier. There were the same buildings, the same cracked and blistered signs, the same saloon bars and the same gambling saloon.

And the ghost town had come to life again. But this time peopled with laughing, chattering sightseers who tried to warm their hard, sophisticated, civilised hearts with an echo of the past.

When we swung off the main drag and wended our way along a tortuous, dusty path leading to Ghost City, I shot another glance at Sally. Her face was set in a sullen stare. It made me feel bitter to see her that way, because we could have had such fun this evening.

And as we got closer, there was a sign that read:

**Ghost City Car Park
First Turning Right**

The signboard was old and weathered, and the characters burned into the wood. And it was peppered with bullet holes, as though Jesse James himself had galloped along this very path and loosed off a volley of shots in derision.

There were already about fifty cars in the corral-like car park, and the attendant looked like something out of a Western film. He slouched over with his thumbs looped in his belt, which hung low over his hips, and the butts of two wicked-looking colts bobbing menacingly at his sides.

But there was something very nineteen-forties-ish in the way he pocketed the parking fee.

Then we entered Ghost City, stumbling along the dusty centre road. The place was all lit up with imitation oil lamps. Smartly dressed fellas with their dames sat out on the sideboards drinking beer and eating sandwiches, while waiters dressed as cow-pokes hefted rough wooden trays.

There was a sing-song coming from one saloon accompanied by a tinny old piano, and further down the street a banjo-accordion band was playing folk dances. An old, bearded Westerner was chanting out the steps of the dance in a monotonous cracked undertone, beating his hands in time with the music while customers laughingly tried to master | the intricate steps of the old-time dances.

'Let's grab a drink,' I said to Sally.

She didn't answer. She just sniffed.

I took her by the arm and marched her up the steps leading to the sideboards. I thrust her against the swinging doors of a saloon and shoved inside.

A lotta fellas and their dames were lined up against the bar, and the rest of the saloon was taken up by card tables. There were all kinds of games in progress: faro, vingt-et-un, poker and banker. A big notice invited anyone to join in and play. At each table there was one man garbed in Western clothes. These men were working for the house. The men and dames playing against them were the suckers who'd come down from town for an evening's fun.

The bartender sidled over to me. 'What'll it be ?'

'Two beers,' I said.

Sally sniffed. She didn't like beers.

'Two beers,' the bartender yelled along the counter. At the far end, another bartender filled two glasses from a cask, and, as he filled them, skimmed them along the shiny surface of the counter. He musta had a lotta practice. As the glasses skimmed along the bar top, they didn't spill one drop of beer, and they were given exactly the right amount of momentum. The glasses stopped right by my elbow.

'Two bucks,' said the bartender.

I raised my eyebrows. But I didn't kick. There were a lotta overheads to carry in this joint. I sipped my beer and watched the card players. I watched pretty closely, and it looked to me like the games were on the level. But you never can tell with cards. I've seen conjurors do things with cards that you'd stake your life on it was impossible to do. Maybe those mock-Western card players were just being careful and not winning too much all at once.

'This is grand fun,' I said to Sally.

She snorted. That was all. And it suddenly struck me that since we'd started out, she hadn't once spoken to me. It gets me the way dames can sulk – and keep on sulking.

But I didn't have much time to think about her, because an argument suddenly started between two of the mock Westerners. It looked pretty serious, too. One of them had tilted back in his chair and overbalanced. He'd sprawled against the man seated at the next table. This fella objected, and to add point to his objection, he took a swing at the other guy.

It musta been just like it was in the old days, because those two men were tough fellas, and they were mad at each other. You could sense how mad they were. A silence settled all over the saloon, folks stopped playing and stared at these two fellas, who were standing facing each other with burning hatred written all over their faces.

They didn't bandy words very much. But what they did say was very much to the point. Things looked ugly. The bartender standing beside me edged nervously toward the far end of the counter.

And then all at once it happened. Those fellas were wearing guns. And they both went for them at the same time. Just for a brief second, I saw what it was like to be quick on the draw. There didn't seem to be much to chose between them for speed. And then shots crashed out and folk ducked and dodged. Through the haze of smoke, I saw one of the mock Westerners sway. And then all at once he tumbled in a heap. He went down so that his body made a loose kinda slumping noise, and his gun slithered across the floor, and you could hear it slithering as plain as plain.

I guess most of the folk there were just struck dumb. They stood like they were paralysed, me along with rest of them, and if anyone had been scattering feathers around, you'd have heard them thudding on the floorboards.

And then, just as the tension was about to break, the fella who'd been shot suddenly sat up with a broad on his face.

Yeah, it was just a bit more atmosphere. A real old-time gun-fight with six-guns and fancy drawing. But there weren't any bodies to shovel earth on to. It was all a good joke. And after folks recovered from the shock, they rocked with an hysterical laughter that showed only too well how much they'd been fooled.

I laughed with the rest of them. It eased the tension that had bubbled up inside me when that fella had slumped down on the floorboards. And the rest of the folk got back to their cards, and the games went on.

And as for Sally. Well, she'd frozen stiff. I guess she'd been looking for a chance to needle. This was it.

'Get me out of this place,' she said. 'It's unbearable.'

'What's the matter, honey? Don't you like a little fun?'

'It's horrible,' she said with a shudder.

'Nonsense. Look; everybody else things it was funny. They've all forgotten about it.'

'I want to go.'

'Drink your beer,' I said.

'I don't want it.'

I took the glass of beer and held it out toward her with the handle facing her so she could take it easily. 'C'mon, honey. Drink your beer,' I urged.

'I don't want it,' she said icily.

'Drink it,' I said, and there was a firmness in my voice that I didn't often use.

Her eyes fenced with mine. And then she reached out and took the glass. But she didn't drink the beer. She tipped the glass slowly so the beer ran all over the floor. She did a proper job of it; upended the glass and then shook it to make sure the last drop fell on the floor. Then she banged the glass back on the counter.

'Satisfied?' she asked.

'Yeah,' I said grimly. 'I'm satisfied.'

I banged on the counter, and the bartender came along to me.

'What's this about a wheel?' I asked.

'Sure,' he said. 'We've got a wheel. It's further down the street, in a saloon on the right-hand side. It's called Hellcat Hole.'

I grunted a thanks, turned away, grabbed Sally by the elbow and practically walker her out of the saloon.

'Leave go my arm,' she protested.

'Shut your nasty little mouth or I'll shut it for you,' I threatened.

She plucked at my fingers, trying to get her arm

free. But she hadn't the strength that I've got. I walked her along the street toward Hellcat Hole, and our shoes made loud, clip-clopping sounds on the sideboards.

'Let me go,' she demanded fiercely.

'Listen, sour-puss, I didn't want you to come tonight. But now you've come, you're gonna wait until I'm ready to go. I'm not gonna start chasing back to town on your account.'

'You swine. I wish I'd never set eyes on you,' she said.

'That goes for me too, sister.'

She tried to twist her arm free. I tightened my fingers so it must have bruised her arm, and she squealed. Then she lapsed into the pained, stony silence that she'd worn around her like a mantle every time we fell out.

I sighed. 'You can still enjoy yourself, honey, if you're sensible.'

Stony silence.

I gave it up. When we got opposite Hellcat Hole, I walked her down the steps and across the dusty street. Another mock Westerner came galloping along the main street. He loosed off a volley of shots in the air and folk scattered out of his way. He reined in hard just by us and tethered his horse outside the Hellcat Hole.

'Howdy pard? 'he yelled at me.

'Howdy,' I grinned back. To be honest, I was rather tickled by all this. Maybe it was because I'd seen so many cowboy and Injun films when I was a kid that this all seemed like a life I useta know.

Sally just glared at him in stony silence, and it me sick to see her act that way.

'All right,' I said. 'Just get up them steps,' and I kinda ran her up the wooden steps on to the sideboards and forced her inside the saloon.

By the time we got inside, she was like a volcano, all pent up and liable to burst her top at any moment. But I wasn't far off blowing my own top either, and whichever way you look at it, we were all set for a blow-up that evening.

I grabbed Sally and walked her straight across the room to where fellas and their dames were grouped around a large table. We got right up close so we could see it good. It was a pukka roulette wheel.

In a vague kinda way, I've always been interested in gambling, purely from a scientific angle. And personally, I've formed the conclusion that gambling is a mug's game. But I've also developed theories about different approaches to gambling.

For example, if you start to gamble and you believe that the game or sport you are gambling upon is crooked, then you have a chance to win. Because all you do then is to ask yourself, 'Who is going to gain financially out of this and how?' and bet alongside the fella who is the answer to your question.

I applied this question to myself regarding the roulette wheel. 'Who,' I asked myself, 'is going to win at this game?' And the answer was that the house was going to win. Why was the house going to win ? Well, because they'd fixed the wheel so that they'd win.

That was a reasonable assumption to make, wasn't it?

I put my theory into practice. I looked over the table and weighed it| up. As far as I could see, if red came up, the banks stood to win the most money.

I put ten dollars on red.

My theory worked. Red came up, and I gathered in twenty dollars. I did the same thing with the next spin, and turned my twenty dollars into forty.

I said to Sally, proudly: 'Look, honey. I got this thing weighed up. Just watch this.'

Sally grunted. But she watched, just the same.

I weighed up the board for the third time. I could see that if red won a third time, the bank would again stand to win, since the amount they'd have to pay out if red won was less than they'd have to pay out if black won, so I plonked down my forty dollars on red and waited.

The mock Westerner who was acting as croupier spun the wheel and then flicked the little white ball into the gully. I watched it as it rolled and bounced against the spinning burr of the numbered holes. And then something caught in my throat. I had just realised something that had been sticking out a mile but that I hadn't seen until just this minute. And now it was too late to do anything about it.

When I'd looked at the board, there'd been two-fifty dollars wagered on black and two-twenty dollars wagered on red. That meant, if red turned up, the bank stood to win thirty dollars. BUT! When I'd put my forty dollars on red, the situation was altered. The bank then stood to lose if red came up. Black had to win, or else the bank would be losing.

When black turned up, I was then quite certain that the wheel was crooked. But that didn't help me any. I'd lost the thirty dollars I'd won and the original ten I'd started with as well.

Sally said: 'Let's go now.'

'Whadya mean, honey. I'm just getting warmed up.'

'For Crissake, Hank,' she said. 'I'm tired, fed up and I want to go home.'

'Have a bet, honey,' I said. 'Have a little bet. It's fun.'

'I don't want to have a bet,' she said.

I pulled out my wallet and began to open it. 'Just one little bet,' I tried to encourage her.

'I said no,' she scowled.

'Just one little bet,' I urged. I was holding my wallet open, and the edges of the bills were showing. Sally said, 'Hell, what do I care,' and snatched at a note sticking out from my wallet. She didn't even look at the note, she just flung it anywhere, somewhere on the table, and as it fluttered down on a number, the croupier called, 'No more bets,' and spun the wheel.

'Hey,' I said, 'That was a century note, you crazy bitch.'

'What do I care?' she flared. 'You wanted me to bet. I have. You got what you wanted.'

I wasn't listening to her. I was looking at the table. The note had fluttered down on to number fourteen. And in case you don't know what that means, I'll tell you. The roulette wheel gives the players a variety of bets. You can bet just red or black, which is an even chance, or else you can bet on groups of numbers, which give you odds of four to one, or three to one or twelve to one.

But that century note had fluttered down on to just one number. And the odds against the number turning up were thirty-seven chances to one. I swallowed hard and watched the little white ball dancing around the bowl of the spinning wheel. I nudged Sally hard and said: 'You crazy little fool, that was a C note.'

'So you're mad about it, now?'

'Sure,' I said. 'I'm mad seeing good dough thrown away like that.'

'All right,' she said ominously. 'I'll give you that hundred bucks back. I don't care if I have to work my fingers to the bone, I'll see you get that hundred back if it's the last thing I do.'

'I'll keep you to that,' I said, and I meant it right then.

Now I'm not short of a few dollars, and a hundred bucks don't mean all that to me. But staking big dough that way looked to me like a sheer waste of dough, and no fella likes to see good dough thrown away, no matter how rich he is.

Sally snorted. 'Now take me home.'

'Go home by yourself,' I said.

'Right, I will.'

My stomach turned over when she began to walk over to the door. She'd been getting me mad, and I was getting fed up with having her around, sulking the way she was. But when it came to her walking out this way, it made me unhappy.

A fella over by the table yelled out suddenly: 'Hey, miss. You gotta take your winnings.'

Sally stopped and turned around. The croupier yelled out again, 'Fourteen wins.'

Sally's face didn't change. She just looked straight at me and then came back to the table. The folk lining the table made way for her, and she stood there with an expressionless face as the croupier, with a sour look on his face, counted out thirty-six C notes.

Sally collected them, casually stuffed them into her handbag, picked up the C note that had been her stake and was still lying on number fourteen and held it out for me to take.

'There's the hundred bucks I owe you,' she said.

'That's okay,' I said. 'You keep it. Have another

whirl; maybe you'll be lucky again.'

She deliberately opened her fingers so that the note fluttered down towards the ground. And I did what every other guy would have done who saw a hundred bucks fluttering down towards the floor. I dived for it.

And when I got erect again, I was just in time to see the saloon doors swinging shut behind Sally.

I stood there for a moment, feeling blue and miserable and undecided what to do. Then I lounged over to the bar and ordered a rye.

I was halfway through the rye when I suddenly realised what she was going to do. She had nearly four the bucks in that handbag of hers. With four thousand bucks, she could go almost any place. And she was in that kinda mood that would make her go almost any place.

Sally and me might not have been getting along so well together just lately. But I wasn't gonna let her walk out that way just on account that we had a few grumbles from time to time.

I didn't even wait to finish the rye. I banged down the glass and skated across the saloon towards the door. There were four or five guys trying to get in at the same time as I tried to get out. But I wasn't wasting time. I kinda scattered them like ninepins, slamming the swing doors open, and the one guy that the door missed, I butted to one side with my shoulder.

I set off, running up the street as hard as I could go. I knew Sally could be awfully stubborn at times, and this was one of the times she was gonna be as stubborn as she knew how.

There was a kinda concerted roar from behind me from the fellas I'd bowled over. But I didn't give them a second thought. All at once, it had come over me how mighty important Sally was to have around me. If I should lose Sally … ! I tucked my elbows into my sides and tried to lengthen my pace.

I was practically all outta breath by the time I reached the car park, and immediately I picked out my car. Sally was backing it out into a position ready to drive off. I went racing across to her, and she saw me. The car attendant was standing there just beside her. She said something to him and he turned around quickly. Something about the way he stood there and then circled around me warned me she'd slipped him a few bucks to hold me off if I looked like trying to get in the way of her exit.

Well, if that was the way it was, I could face up to that.

I ran straight at the fella. I was going at a good speed, and I'm a pretty hefty kinda guy. That mock Westerner was gonna need to have a lotta stamina to hold me back.

I ran straight at him, and I was in the mood to run straight through him. I wasn't afraid of being hurt, and the way things were, I reckoned he'd get hurt a good deal more than I'd be.

I hurtled at him. I felt I had the speed of a bullet. I felt I'd hit him and smack him right outta my path like an express train will shove a cow off the line.

I saw the guy tensed for the impact, hurtling towards me, and I bunched both my hands together like a battering ram that would dig a great hole in his face.

And just at the last minute, he seemed to disappear. What he actually did was to double himself up and roll himself at my legs. From all points of view, that was the best thing he coulda done anyway. The most harm he suffered that way was a ribful of my feet, and any tough guy can stand up to a few kicks in the ribs.

But what it did to me!

Just imagine your own head and shoulders travelling along at a great speed, and then your legs being unable to catch up with them.

I made a perfect pancake landing. My chest, hands and chin all hit the dust at the same time. And I hit the ground really hard. I hit it so hard, I was jarred through and through, and by the time I got over the shock of it and climbed unsteadily to my feet, Sally had got into gear. She shot past me with a whoosh that nearly took me with her.

I stood there unsteadily, gazing after the rapidly retreating rear light of my car, realising dimly that Sally was going away from me and that she'd left me there without a car, so I would have to bum my way home the best way I could.

'So yuh think yore tough, do you?' said a voice behind me.

I turned around. It was the car park attendant. He was looking ugly, and his hands hung by his sides threateningly.

'On ya way, fella,' I said tiredly.

'Shoving dames around,' he grumbled. 'Ya oughta keep them hands of yores tired to yore sides.'

I lost my temper then. Sally had left me flat, and this guy had stopped me from preventing her from going. Moreover, to add insult to injury, Sally had taken my car, and this guy was supposed to be looking after cars. He got good dough for seeing the wrong guys didn't take the wrong cars.

For a moment all I could see was his long chin jutting out at me aggressively. And then I didn't see it any more. But my knuckles were singing with pain.

The fella lay there in the dust for quite a time. When he climbed to his feet, he was groggy.

'Wanna say anything more about it?' I invited menacingly.

He rubbed his chin, glared at me, but kept a good distance from me.

I fumbled in my pocket, produced my car park ticket and flung it at him. 'That's my car you just let outta here,' I told him.

'But the dame said …' he protested.

'Oh go take a jump in the lake.'

I looked at the other cars speculatively, wondering if maybe I could chance grabbing one off the line and chasing Sally, or maybe getting some kind-hearted guy to drive me to town so I could head off Sally. But before I could make up my mind which line of action to adopt, I heard angry voices behind me. I turned around. Five men who'd just entered the car park had broken into a run. They were all looking at me, and I had the uneasy feeling they were competing among themselves to get at me first.

I could tell right away they were after my blood. And my mind went clicking back over the past few minutes, reminding me that I'd blasted outta that saloon at a hell of a lick and scattered five guys who were just coming in to have a drink.

I didn't have to recognise them to know these were the five guys. And I didn't have to wait until I got walloped before I'd know they were after my blood.

It was flight or fight, and the odds got me stubborn. I squared my shoulders and waited.

The first guy made a swing at my jaw. I let that slip over my shoulder and sunk my fist in his belly. He doubled up quickly like a spring, and the next fella stumbled over him, which gave me a chance to clip him over the ear.

The third guy landed a fist on my temple and squashed my nose. I roared, shook my head and struck out all round. I vaguely realised that there were guys all around me now, swinging blows, yelling and breathing down the back of my neck. And I was taking punishment now. I had a slight advantage. Whenever I hit out and contacted, it was sure to hit somebody I was fighting. But these five guys were hitting each other as much as they hit me.

Maybe it was a good safety-valve for the trouble I'd been having with Sally. I was getting a wild kinda exhilarating feeling, standing there, hitting out all round, taking punishment but nevertheless keeping on my feet and giving at least as good as I got.

But I'd been forgetting about the car-park attendant. I'd given him a nasty jolt, and he didn't like it. Furthermore, he was standing right behind me when the trouble started. I shouldn't have forgotten about him, because then he wouldn't have been able to slug me in the back of the neck with his bunched fists. It kinda paralysed me for a moment, and I felt my knees give way so that I sank down. And another fist came out from somewhere and slammed against my jaw.

The night exploded into sparks that died out one by one, very slowly, but very surely, leaving just the black of night.

3

When I got around to consciousness again, there were a coupla fellas slapping my face and spilling whisky down my throat.

I coughed as the strong spirit burned my throat, and then bleared up at them through half-closed eyes.

'How d'ya feel, buddy?'

I propped myself up on my elbows and looked around The car park was almost empty. There was no sign of the five fellas that had attacked me, and the car park attendant seemed to have disappeared also.

'What happened to them?' I asked.

'What happened to who?'

'There were five of them,' I told him. 'But the car park keeper socked me from behind.'

One guy looked at the other. There was a wise look in his eyes. He said: 'You musta gotta bit mixed up, fella. The attendant helped you when those guys set on you.'

'Where's he gone to?'

'He's cleared off. Had to get home on account his wife is sick.'

'Gimme a hand, willya?'

They helped me to my feet, and I stood there

leaning on one of them. My jaw was sore like it had been worked loose in its socket and one of my eyes wouldn't open properly.

'How long have I been out?'

'Maybe fifteen minutes.'

I swore softly. Fifteen minutes' start would be all that Sally would need. I knew what she'd do. She'd go back to the hotel, dump my car, get her bags and scram.

'Well, thanks a lot, you fellas,' I said.

'That's okay. Always ready to help. Can you drop you somewhere?'

'Sure. I gotta get back to the Metropole. Pretty urgent, too.'

'That's swell. We pass right by there.'

My legs musta got twisted in the struggle, and it caused me a bit of pain as we walked over to their car. I had to limp. When I got settled down in the back of the car, the fella who was driving said:

'Lose any dough, buddy?'

I hadn't thought of that. I fumbled in my pocket, but my wallet was still intact.

'No,' I said. 'They didn't roll me.'

'Maybe they had a grudge against you? 'said the other man, and there was a question in his voice.

I didn't feel like answering questions. I was burning the seat of my pants with impatience. I just wanted to find out what had happened to Sally.

'Maybe,' I said. And the way I said it stopped any more questions being asked.

They dropped me off at the Metropole, and as soon as I got inside, I could tell by the way the reception clerk looked at me that Sally had scrammed.

I went straight over to him. 'What's on your mind?' I asked.

He looked uncomfortable and shuffled his feet.

'Nothing,' he mumbled. 'That is, I expect you know that …'

'Did she leave a message?' I asked bluntly.

'Only that you'd settle the bill.'

'Sure. But did she say where she was going?'

He shook his head emphatically.

I said: 'I'll give you double what she gave you to shut your trap, if you'll start talking right now.'

'Well,' he stammered. He looked at me, looked at the desk, then looked down behind the desk at his feet.

'Whad'ya know?' I said.

'She checked out to another hotel.'

'Howd'ya know?'

'She asked me to recommend another hotel.'

'Yeah. And what makes you think she took your tip?'

He looked uncomfortable again.

I said: 'Because she gave you dough to keep your mouth shut?'

'Ten bucks,' he told me. 'She had to find somewhere, and it ain't that easy to find hotels this time of night. I knew the fella at the other hotel, and he fixed her up on the phone right here before she left.'

I got out my wallet, peeled a twenty note off my wad and flicked it across the counter at him. 'Spill it,' I said.

'You ain't gonna let on I backed down on her?'

'Naw. You earned your dough both times.'

'It's the Premont Hotel,' he said. 'It's over on Creol Avenue.'

I said: 'Okay, get my bill ready, I'm checking out.'

'Sure,' he said.

'But you'd better get your buddy on the phone and

make sure he's got a room for me at the Premont.'

It was getting late; nearly one o'clock by the time I trundled my bags into the Premont. A few discreetly distributed dollar bills got my bags up to my room and gave me the low-down on Sally's room-number.

I waited until there was nobody around in the corridor and then went up to Sally's room. I knuckled the door.

She said cautiously, through the shut door: 'Who's that?'

I didn't answer; I just knuckled again urgently, imperatively.

She opened the door. I knew she would. No woman could resist opening a door when someone knocks that way. She opened it only a coupla inches. But that was good enough for me. I turned those two inches into two feet with a good shove, and was inside before she even recognised me. I shut the door behind me and leaned against it.

'Know me? I'm the bad penny.'

'Get out,' she said, in a voice so low I could barely hear it. But she spoke low because she was having difficulty in suppressing her fury.

'Look, Sally,' I said, trying to be reasonable, 'let's stop biting each other's head off.'

She had five fingers on her right hand. Each and every separate finger burned an impression on my cheek. And the back of my head banged against the door.

'Now will you get out?' she mouthed.

This wasn't the Sally I knew. This girl was a stranger. A woman who hated me with every fibre in her being. I just couldn't believe it could happen. We'd been pals; good pals. We'd had our quarrels, we'd had our grievances. But this …!

'You pack a wallop,' I said. 'Okay, you've let off steam now, and maybe I did deserve that. Now let's talk things over.' I made like I was gonna take her by the arm and steer her inside.

I got a slap around the face that time that made me see stars. It also made me see red. I was prepared to be reasonable. But I wasn't prepared to be slapped around like that by anybody, dame or no dame.

'All right, you've asked for it,' I said.

I moved in quickly. She slapped with the other hand, but I took that on my arm. I shoulda followed up by grabbing her, but I thought she'd start swinging again, and I got ready to block it.

But Sally had sense. She didn't swing at me again. She turned and ran. I ran after her, along the short corridor and through into the bedroom.

I entered the room just in time to meet the chair she'd skimmed across the floor. The chair tangled with my legs and I hit the carpet with a thump.

By the time I'd scrambled to my feet, she'd got down the house phone and was screaming blue murder into the mouthpiece.

'Yeah,' she said. 'Get that house dick up here quick. There's a crazy guy trying to get fresh.'

She broke off and swung a vase at me. I dodged and it smashed against the wall behind me.

'Quick,' she yelled. 'He's coming for me again.'

I stood there feeling like a dope while she replaced the receiver.

'It'll take that dick about a minute to get up here,' she said. 'Now will you get out?'

I looked at her steadily. This wasn't working out the way I'd figured, not even a little bit. I'd hoped we'd talk, argue, apologise and then bill and coo. But I could tell by the look in her eyes that she'd just as soon see me dying slowly in torment.

'Okay,' I said. 'If that's the way you want it.'

'That's the way I want it,' she said.

I walked out. I walked out with a jaunty step, but I was feeling miserable as hell. I reached the end of the corridor as the elevator doors began to open.

I didn't wait to see the house dick or to hear the story that Sally had to tell. I was pretty certain she wouldn't say anything that would get me turfed outta the hotel. But that wasn't much consolation.

I got back to my room, opened my suitcase and took out the bottle of Scotch I carried around for company. I tilted a large dose into the toothbrush glass, sprayed it with a shot from the basin tap and drank it down like it was beer.

Then I poured out another liberal dose, unwatered this time, kicked off my shoes and lay on the bed. My face was still smarting from the wallop she'd handed me. But that was nothing to the smart I was feeling inside.

I felt like hell. And the crazy thing was, I couldn't understand why I was feeling so bad. All day we'd been bickering, and Sally had sulked, and I'd wished her to hell. But now everything was all set for me to walk out on the dame, I didn't wanna walk out. In fact, I was feeling so low I coulda crawled under a postage stamp stuck to the floorboards.

I guess every fella's a sucker for a dame at some time or another. I guess I was a sucker for Sally. I switched the light out after a time and lay there in the dark, remembering all the things about Sally that I liked, forgetting all the things about her that I didn't like, and screwing the heart outta myself so I felt I coulda cried.

The thing that hurt more than anything was the realisation that she'd suddenly begun to hate me. There was a transparent barrier she'd erected between us that was twenty feet high and just as broad. I couldn't get at her through that barrier. I could see the real Sally all right. I could see the Sally I wanted, the Sally who talked and laughed and sang with me. But she wasn't singing any more. And she'd become like a stranger; somebody I didn't know. Trying to talk to Sally was like fiddling around with a crystal set and trying to get a station you knew was there but you just couldn't tune in.

. I gave up all hope of sleeping, poured myself another large Scotch and felt it run down into my belly, like stream of burning acid. But it wasn't having any effect upon my mind. I was stone-cold sober.

I got up, switched on the light, lit the twentieth cigarette and began to pace the room in a kinda dumb misery that nothing could ease. I deliberately refused to think of the next day. The next day could mean the end of Sally as far as I was concerned. She could be up and away in the morning, and she could chose North, East, South or West to travel. And unless I spied on her, I'd never know where she went. She'd have slid outta my life forever, like a dime rolling down a main street drain.

There was a radio fitted in the room. I switched that on and did some more pacing.

A familiar voice said softly: 'And now, folks, it's just three o'clock, and for those with memories, it's 'Three O'Clock in the Morning' played by Ben Ross and his Accordion Revellers.'

I paced up and down. The radio softly purred its message to the still wakeful folk who were enduring the hours until daybreak. From time to time, the familiar voice of the announcer chimed in, wisecracking, commenting, being cheerful and introducing the records as he played them.

It musta been many sleepless hours later when something that had been nagging at the back of my mind began to get a grip on me. That announcer's voice. Why should it be familiar? This was Oklahoma. The radio station was one of many operating in this district. And I'd never been to this district previously.

So the next time the announcer spoke, I listened carefully. I knew that voice. It was a cheery but deep voice that seemed to suggest wide open space and healthiness.

Yes, I was quite sure now. I knew the voice, recognised the intonation. I listened for its rise and fall and anticipated every hidden chuckle in the voice.

But I couldn't nail it down. I couldn't remember to whom the voice belonged. Trying to remember who owned that voice was like chasing a butterfly. I just couldn't find a face in my memory to attach the voice to. And that could have been because I'd never met the owner of the voice. Maybe I'd just seen him in the films or maybe on the stage. Yet somehow I knew the voice too intimately for it to have been just a film voice.

Then I switched back to thinking about Sally again, and when I did, it was like the whole world had become grey and empty. Sally was there in that hotel. But she mighta been a million miles away or even dead for all the comfort that give me. Because I knew from the way she had looked at me and the way she had spoken that I meant nothing to her – probably less than nothing. All that had meant anything to us was now finished.

The grey light of morning was beginning to flush out the dark night. The ashtray was littered with stubs and the bottle of Scotch lay on its side, empty. I still paced the room in my stockinged feet, feeling like hell, with a sickness deep down inside me and a lump that needed only a momentary relaxation of control before it leaped into my throat.

And suddenly I felt stifled. I just had to get outta that hotel and get some fresh air. Maybe Sally would be packing to clear off somewhere. Well, I couldn't stop her going. I just didn't wanna be around when she did go. That would hurt too much.

I washed up a bit at the basin. The radio was still crooning away. I cleaned my teeth thoroughly, because my mouth tasted like the floor of a chicken run. My feet had swollen while I'd been pacing up and down, and it was a job to squeeze them into my shoes. I didn't dare pull the laces tight.

I grabbed my hat and walked over to the radio to switch it off. Just as I did so, the announcer said: 'How're you doin' folks ? Five o'clock now. Are you tired like I am? I've been playing these records for five hours now. Only half an hour longer and yours truly, Victor Lane, will be signing off ...'

I didn't listen to any more, because the face clicked in line with the voice. Victor Lane! I knew Victor Lane right enough. We'd been buddies in New York. He'd been a scriptwriter then, writing vaudeville shows for radio.

I clicked off the radio and walked over to the door. Then I stopped. Victor Lane! He'd be through in half an hour. Why not pick him up at the radio station? I wanted somebody to jolt me outta the depression I was in. He'd be the fella to do it.

There were a coupla telephone books by the bedside. I thumbed through until I found the address of the radio station he was working for, and I quit the place in a hurry. I had only half an hour to get there, and it was over on the other side of the town.

4

I got there exactly three minutes before Victor was due off the air. A sleepy-eyed attendant in the reception hall showed me a chair and asked me to wait.

I didn't have to wait more than ten minutes, and then Victor Lane came busting out through the swing doors leading to the relay stations.

'Hank,' he yelled. 'Gee, boy, it's good to see ya.'

He pumped my hand up and down and it made me feel good to be there with him. There was something warm and invigorating in his make-up that made me feel better.

I looked him over. He seemed bigger than I ever remembered him being, and he was sporting a walrus moustache, of the type that the fellas in the British RAF use. His eyes grinned and twinkled mischievously and one eyebrow arched itself whenever he spoke.

'Oklahoma agrees with you,' I said.

'Anywhere agrees with me. If it don't, I make it agree.' He laughed infectiously and his eyebrows arched.

Then he introduced me to a slim young fella with black hair plastered down over his head. 'Meet Jimmy Chark,' he said.

I shook hands with Jimmy, and his white teeth flashed a welcome. I liked his eyes; they were brown eyes, thoughtful and kindly eyes.

'Pleased to meecher,' he said.

'That goes for me, too.'

Victor put one burly arm around my shoulders. 'I'm going for a steak and egg,' he said. 'What say you come join us?'

'Why d'ya think I'm here?'

'What are we waiting for then?'

We went across the road to an all-night café. Apparently Victor was a regular customer there. His steak and egg was waiting for him, cooked and smelling delicious. Me and Jimmy had to wait for ours to be cooked.

'Whatya doing here?' Victor demanded, his mouth full of grub.

'Just looking around,' I said. 'Heard your show last night, recognised your voice and came on over.'

Victor pointed his knife at Jimmy. 'He's half the show,' he said, and swallowed a mouthful of steak that shoulda choked him.

I looked enquiringly at Jimmy. He grinned. 'I put on the records,' he said.

'He's smart,' said Victor. 'He don't make no mistakes, ever. Always puts on the right record and always the right side.'

'That's easy,' said Jimmy. 'I've got the easy side of it. I'd hate to do all the gabbing you do. Talking all through the night to folk you can't see.'

'Waste of time, isn't it?' I asked.

Victor shook his head and grinned. He wasn't annoyed that I should be thinking he was wasting his time. 'You ain't got no idea, Hank. We reckon there must be fifty thousand folks listen in all night.'

'Are there that many guys with something on their conscience in Oklahoma?'

'There are nightworkers,' said Jimmy. 'Think of all the nightworkers, watchmen, garage hands, all-night cafés, factories, fellas with insomnia, folk who have to get up at three in the morning to go to work. Don't you get it wrong, fella. Any time you wanna say during the night, there's fifty thousand folk on the other end of that mike.'

It had never occurred to me before that there'd be all them folk listening all through the night.

Victor pointed out: 'You were one of the fifty thousand tonight.'

'Sure,' I said. 'But that was different. I had something on my mind.'

Victor looked at Jimmy and grinned. It was like they had a secret joke between them.

'What goes on? 'I demanded, looking from one to the other of them.

Jimmy explained. 'It's like a mad house in that radio station,' he said. 'Folks keep ringing in all night. Some want us to play this record or that record, others threaten us with all kinds of torture if we don't stop broadcasting what they call rubbish.'

'And you answer the telephone?'

'In between playing the records,' said Jimmy. 'And we get some queer customers on the phone, too.'

'Maybe I shoulda rung you instead of coming down here?'

'At least you'd have been a pleasant surprise,' said Victor.

'Ain't some of them pleasant?'

Jimmy said: 'What would you do? There's a fella

that's gonna sling himself outta window five stories high on account some dame has passed him up. So just before he tries to fly, he rings us on the telephone, sobs his heart out and asks us to play 'Forever in My Heart,' so he can die happy, remembering that his dame useta like this song.'

I remembered that I coulda been doing just that thing myself if I'd had just a little less self-control. I said: 'Are there folks who are that screwy?'

'It's happening all the time,' he said. 'But what would you have done?'

I thought about it. 'That's his business,' I said. 'Maybe he wasn't gonna jump anyway.'

'Victor fixed it,' said Jimmy. 'He talky-talked with the guy. The guy was anxious to talk, too. Told Victor what she looked like, what she wore and what her aunt said about the way she dressed. Him and Victor sure did have a heart to heart talk.'

'And Victor talked him outta jumping,' I guessed.

'Naw,' drawled Jimmy. 'You can't talk nuts like that outta what they're gonna do. I got to work on the other phone, told the cops, they traced the call, and he was still talking on the phone to Victor when they busted into his flat and put the arm on him.'

'So you save lives too, eh?'

'It's all in the service,' said Victor.

We'd finished eating by this time, and we went over to the counter and grabbed ourselves another coffee apiece. As we stood there talking, a young, fresh-faced fella of about twenny-two ambled in, threw his hat on a hat-rack and came over to the counter.

Victor said: 'Howya Flash? What's hot this morning?'

Flash grinned uncomfortably. 'Can't you drop this

Flash business?'

Victor grinned at me and thumbed towards Flash. 'This fella's a reporter, Hank. Leastways, that's what he says he is. But nobody ain't sure what he is yet; they've never been able to get his diapers stripped off him.'

'Shuddup, you big-faced baboon,' said Flash.

Victor playfully cuffed his head. 'You know why he's called Flash?' he asked. 'He's the guy they sent out one night to get a story on a reported oil strike. He came back with the story the next day, seventeen hours after the rest of the papers had given the same story headline build-up.'

Flash growled. 'Everybody knows what happened. I got a hot lead on something else.'

'Which turned out to be colder than an iceberg.'

Jimmy asked: 'What's special this morning, Flash?'

'Papers will be out any time now.'

Victor said: 'Just in case you've never met a real reporter, kid, get a load of our friend here, Hank Janson. He's covered some of the toughest assignments New York can dish out.'

I said: 'Can it, Victor.'

Flash said: 'Gee, have you been on a New York paper?'

'Forget it,' I told him. 'It's ancient history. I'm leading a quiet life now. I wanna forget the bad things in my life.'

'Gee,' he said. 'I'd give my ears to get on a New York paper.'

'If you're ever silly enough to wanna go that far, kid,' I told him, 'it'll cost you more than your ears. It'll probably cost you twenty years of your life.'

We were standing up by the counter, sipping at our coffee, which had been really hot, and there was nobody else there except for the café proprietor, who was in the back, washing some dishes.

The door swung open, but none of us took any notice until a voice said: 'Say, you're Sid Gordon, aincher?'

Flash turned round. We all did. The fella who had spoken was short and squat with a bulbous nose. There was another fella with him. A taller fella with thin lips and eyes that were slits.

Flash said: 'Yeah, I'm Sid Gordon.'

The squat fella moved right up close to him, and the tall guy kept right beside him.

Squatty pushed his face forward so it was only inches from Flash's face. 'I gotta message for you,' he said.

Flash looked mystified. His fresh, round face looked quite boyish. 'Who from?' he said.

'From a fella that don't like the articles you've been writing recently.'

'Yeah? What's the message?'

'This,' said Squatty, and all at once he seemed to be greased lightning. His ham-like fist stabbed out and sunk deep into Flash's groin, and as the kid doubled up in pain, and his face came down, Squatty's knee jolted up, flattening the kid's nose and arching him over backwards. There was a squelching sound as flesh and bone were pulped, and blood spattered the floor as it gouted from the place where the kid's nose useta be. The kid sprawled backwards onto the floor, and Squatty drew back his boot and planted it right in the centre of the kid's face.

All this had happened so quickly that it was over before we realised it. Victor was quicker off the mark than me. He swung a left at Squatty that caught the side of his head and caused him to stumble. He was gonna follow this up, but the tall fella moved up. Victor was in my way and I couldn't see what happened. But Victor staggered back with his hand to his face just as I sensed movement from the tall guy.

I tried to get round Victor but cannoned into Jimmy, who was trying to do the same thing. And Squatty and his pal seemed to melt outta the door.

Victor was swearing and holding his face. I could see blood spilling out between his fingers. I looked at the still swinging door, undecided if I should chase after Squatty and his pal or go to Victor's help.

Jimmy said: 'Leave them, Hank. We'll get after them later. I'm worried about Victor.'

Victor had been a very lucky guy. He'd been slashed with a razor. And the beginning of the slash was on his bottom eyelid and it ran right down to his chin. Half an inch higher and the razor would have cleaved his eyeball in two. As it was he had a wound in his cheek that looked like a bleeding mouth that wouldn't stop bleeding.

I held the lips of the wound together while Jimmy got the café proprietor to ring for a doctor. Victor was moaning and swearing. I kept telling him to shut his mouth.

'Just a scratch,' I told him.

'Scratch, my Aunt Jeroma,' he said. 'It's gone right through my cheek. It's bleeding inside my mouth too.' And to prove it he spat blood out on the floor.

'Shut your trap,' I said. 'How can I stop this bleeding when you keep wriggling your face around?'

Jimmy came back. He went white when he saw the amount of blood Victor was losing. 'Can I do anything?' he asked.

'Sure, take over from me, willya? My fingers are getting stiff. I'll take a looksee at the kid.'

When I got over to the kid, he looked bad. His face was a mask of blood, and bubbles of blood formed on his lips as he breathed. I got a bowl of water and cleaned off the blood. He didn't look so bad then. His nose was bent around a bit, and I got hold of it and pulled it straight. The bone gave a nasty grating noise, but the kid was out, and it was better to do this now while he was unconscious than when he came around. I ran my fingers down the bone of his nose and could feel two distinct breaks. I moulded again and then stepped back to survey my handiwork. His nose looked straight enough now except just at the tip, where it had a very slight twist to the left.

Well, he was lucky. If the broken bones started knitting together the way they were, he wouldn't have suffered too badly.

I got out my hip flask and fed him some rye. After a time he began to make noises. He was swallowing a lotta blood, and a lotta blood was dribbling out from his mouth. He'd got a haemorrhage inside at the back, where the nose was joined on. But after a time that stopped.

By this time the doctor had arrived. The doors of the café had been closed and he was getting to work on Victor with stitches.

'Hold it,' the doctor said, 'this is the last one.'

Just as he spoke, Flash's eyes opened. 'How d'ya feel, kid?' I asked.

He looked at me dazedly, and raised a hand towards his nose. It musta been hurting him pretty bad. I grabbed his hand and pulled it back to his side. 'Your nose is okay, kid. Just don't pull it around until the bone has set.'

I saw memory return to him. His eyes showed a glint of fear as h recalled the fist driving into his guts. He looked around apprehensively.

'They've gone,' I said. 'Let's see if you can walk.'

I got my- hands under his armpits and helped him to his feet. He stood there unsteadily, resting one hand on the counter. He looked a real mess. Blood had clotted on his shirt and run down the front of his grey suit.

'Why did they do that?' he asked weakly.

'Forget it for a while, kid. And don't touch that nose of yours, if you wanna keep it straight.' I turned him around so he could see his reflection in the mirror behind the counter. He looked at himself in disgust.

Then he caught sight of the doctor bending over Victor. 'What's that?' he said.

'Victor got cut up a bit. He kinda horned in when those guys waded into you.'

'He ain't hurt?' he said, and made like he was gonna walk over to him.

I held him back with my arm. 'He won't die, kid. In a minute or two, we'll be able to get outta here. Better let the doc look you over first.'

When the doctor was through with Victor, I called him over and he made a rapid examination of Flash.

'You'll be all right,' he said eventually. 'Better get yourself a nose-truss to wear in bed at nights if you wanna stay pretty.'

Victor lounged over. A strip of sticking plaster stretched across his face, blood had dripped all over his clothes, and his face had gone white from the blood he'd lost. But he'd got that cheerful smile of his spread right across his puss.

'How d'ya feel, Flash ? 'he asked.

Flash swallowed, looked at Victor and said: 'Jeepers, you asking me how I am!'

'It's nothing,' Victor replied. He grinned at me. 'Ask Hank. He'll tell you. It's just a scratch.'

Jimmy said: 'Let's get outta here. Let's get some place where you can take it easy, Victor.'

'Sure,' said Vic. 'Let's go up to my flat.'

I said: 'Me and Jimmy have got work to do. You take the kid with you, Victor. We'll be along later.'

Victor looked at me steadily for long moments. Then he said heavily: 'We'll go up to my place first.'

'Yeah, but there's ...'

He interrupted me. 'Quit arguing, Hank. Let's get up to my flat.'

I didn't argue no more. And the four of us called a cab and went off down town to Victor's flat.

5

When we got up to Victor's flat we settled ourselves down while Victor opened up his cocktail cabinet. He had a fine brand that was just what I wanted to loosen up the stiffness inside me caused by the sleepless night I'd had and the excitement of the last hour.

Flash was still white-faced and very, very nervous. Victor, on the other hand, had completely recovered from what musta been a very nasty shock, to say nothing of the loss of blood he'd endured.

'Look, Victor,' I said. 'I don't know what's in your mind, but I reckon this is a job for the cops.'

His eyebrows arched. 'How long you been in Oklahoma, Hank?'

'Two days.'

'Yeah.' He looked down at his glass, and his brow puckered.

'You ain't been here long enough yet to know how the cops are fixed around this neighbourhood.'

'It takes big business to buy cops,' I said. 'A coupla tough hoods like those two wouldn't have that kinda dough.'

Victor looked at Flash. 'What series of articles you

been writing, kid?'

'Ghost City series,' Flash said. A look of understanding came into his eyes. 'Say, you don't think …?'he began.

'Cripes,' said Victor, and his eyes rolled heavenwards, despairingly.

I said: 'Look, I'm a stranger around here. What's all this about a Ghost City series?'

Flash said: 'You know Ghost City?'

I nodded.

'Well, I got an assignment to write up Ghost City. My chief said it's gotta be exposed. It's a vice town.'

'So you've been knocking gambling and what goes on at Ghost City?'

'That's it.'

'And so two fellas come along and give you a work-over on account they don't like the way you write.'

'Yeah. That's the way it looks. But it's kinda difficult to believe.'

Victor said: 'Why's it so difficult to believe?'

Flash swallowed. 'Well, Jegger's a pretty important citizen. Maybe he does own Ghost City. But that's a long way short of hiring hoods to go around smacking guys down.'

Victor chuckled. 'You've got a lot to learn, sonny.'

Jimmy spoke for the first time. 'Jegger don't level out with me as being the kinda guy to hire thugs.'

Victor looked at him. 'Maybe you're biased,' he said.

'Maybe I am. But I still think Jegger's a straight guy.'

I burst in. 'Look, will somebody put me wise? I don't know what you're talking about.'

'I'll bring you up to date,' said Victor. 'Ghost City

is owned and run by a fella named Jegger. And Ghost City is just about the blackest spot you could find in any town, Chicago included. Gambling is just one of the things that goes on in Ghost City. All vices are catered for. Any businessman that's wanting distraction can find it down in Ghost City: blondes, brunettes and red-heads. A hop-head can find himself a skinful of dope, too.'

'And the cops are squared? 'I asked.

'Naturally. Ghost City pays off good dividends, and the cops collect their whack. That's how the wheels go around in any city.'

'An' Jegger is a big shot around town?' I wanted to know.

'That's what makes these two fellas think Jegger can't be employing strong-arm men,' said Victor

Flash said: 'He's on the Council. He couldn't risk anything like that.'

'He risks criticism by owning and running Ghost City,' Victor pointed out.

Flash couldn't help but agree.

Jimmy stretched his long legs. His solemn brown eyes looked at me thoughtfully, and when he spoke, his teeth flashed. 'Jegger is a right guy,' he said. 'Any guy that does the good he does is a right guy.'

Victor said: 'Jimmy's got a soft spot for Jegger on account of the work he does in the reservations.'

'You mean Injun reservations?' I asked.

'Yeah,' said Jimmy. 'And Jegger has made himself a pretty likeable fella for what he does. He's always sending food and stuff up there, and teachers to get to work on the kids and teach them a trade, and nurses and doctors to make sure they're fit and well.'

I gave Jimmy another look. A keen look. His hair was jet black, his eyes brown and his teeth white. His skin was not quite so white as most folks' skin.

I asked: 'What did you say your name was, Jimmy?'

'Chark, Jimmy Chark. And you don't have to form conclusions, because I'm telling you right away that you're right. I'm a tiny part of the old Chocktaw tribe. There been a few generations of white blood in my veins, but there's good Indian blood in me too.'

'That's why he's so interested in the reservations,' said Victor.

Jimmy lit a cigarette and puffed smoke towards the ceiling. 'There's a lot of Indian blood scattered around Oklahoma,' he said. 'Most of the Indian lads on the reservation come out into public life when they've reached the age of eighteen. But some of them are stick-in-the-muds. They won't come out from the reservations. They stay there, living the old way of life that they've always lived. The world grows and develops while they stand still. They're living up there in the reservation exactly as they lived a hundred years ago, cooking on camp fires, living in tepees, and dying off like flies because they haven't the faintest idea of what elementary hygiene and sanitation mean.'

'And that's where Jegger comes in?' I said.

He nodded. 'I'm an American citizen. But I still don't that those folk up there in the reservation are kinsfolk of mine. Anybody who tries to help them is okay by me.'

'I can understand how you feel, Jimmy. But if Jegger is running Ghost City and it's all that I'm told it is, he could still be the kinda guy that'd use thugs.'

'Maybe,' said Jimmy. But his jaw jutted obstinately.

'Those Injun wallahs are all the same,' said Victor. They're as obstinate as hell. I don't know why the hell I have an Injun kicking his heels around my radio show.'

Jimmy grinned. He knew Victor was kidding.

'What about that scar you're gonna wear in future?' I said to Victor.

His face became serious. 'I don't like it, Hank. And when I don't like something, I usually do something about it.'

'Such as?'

'Getting back at Jegger. Flash is just a kid. He'd better lay off those articles in the paper like those fellas told him. But papers ain't the only way to give publicity.'

'You mean the radio!'

'Sure,' he said. 'I'll start an attack on Jegger and force his hand.'

'That may be tough,' I said. 'Maybe you want a scar the other side of your face just to make it look symmetrical.'

'Naw,' he drawled. 'I just wanna see you get scratched for a change.'

'I don't like being scratched with a razor.'

He arched his eyebrow and looked at me thoughtfully. 'You mean you want me to deal you out of this hand?'

I looked at Jimmy, I looked at Flash. I thought of Sally and the bleak days that lay ahead of me. I said: 'Hell, let's see what kind of trumps Jegger can produce anyway.'

6

Guys who sit up and broadcast all night have to sleep sometime. So I left Victor, Jimmy and Flash to grab themselves some shut-eye and spent the rest of the morning and the afternoon wandering around. I was dog-tired and feeling like I was suffering from half a dozen hangovers.

When I got back to the hotel for dinner I saw Sally sitting up at the bar. But she wasn't alone. She had a tall, bronzed, handsome fella with her. He had slick black hair smoothed down over his head, which made me dislike him on sight, and he laughed too much, showing his beautiful, white teeth.

I went over to them, put my arm in between them to rest my hand on the counter while I waited for a drink. The handsome guy looked up and treated me to an indignant look. I glared back at him and he dropped his eyes.

But Sally didn't look up. She'd seen my hand and she was startled when she recognised nay signet ring. But she had sufficient will-power not to look up.

I said quietly: 'How are yuh doing, Sally?'

She looked along the bar away from me as though

she hadn't heard.

I said more loudly: 'I said, how are yuh doing, Sally?'

It was like talking to a marble statue. The bronzed fella was looking at me again. I could feel his eyes boring into me.

'Look, Sally,' I said. 'Maybe you're right. Maybe things aren't the way we thought they were. Maybe we're not suited to each other. But that don't stop us being pals, does it?'

The little wretch wouldn't even glance round at me. The bartender brought my drink, and I paid for it. But I still stood there. The bronzed fella fidgeted awkwardly.

I said: 'You don't have to act like I'm poison, Sally. We tried it out and it didn't work. But we can still be pals.'

The bronzed fella pushed hack his stool and stood up. He cleared his throat and said, 'Sally.'

'Yes, darling?' She turned around at once and smiled at him. She acted like I wasn't standing there.

'D'you know this fella?'

'I don't want to,' she said.

'Look, Sally. All I want is to shake hands and say we're pals. I'm sorry for any unhappiness I've caused you. But let's be pals.'

The bronzed guy tapped me on the shoulder. 'Scram fella, you ain't wanted around here.'

I'd been expecting something like this to happen. It had to happen if I was gonna stand there talking to Sally.

I turned around slowly. 'Take it easy, Handsome,' I said. 'I gotta little matter I wanna talk over with this young lady.'

Handsome pulled his lips back in a grin to show

his teeth. They were nice teeth and he had a pretty smile. But there was menace in his smile. 'Sure, fella. You wanna talk to the lady. But the lady don't wanna talk to you. So what do you do now?'

'You tell me,' I said. 'I'm anxious to know what I do next.'

He was still smiling. 'You do like I said. You scram. That's what you do, fella.'

I looked at him. Then I looked at Sally. 'What about it, Sally. We've had our time together. Let's round it off nicely. Let's be good pals.'

She didn't answer.

Her boyfriend said: 'Do you want this bum here, sweetheart?'

'He's annoying me,' she said.

Handsome said: 'On your way, fella.'

I turned and faced him squarely. I looked him up and down. He was tall, he was powerful and he was athletic. But there was something in his face that made me think that although he had the strength for a rough and tumble, he hadn't the guts to carry it through.

'If you wanna keep your face pretty the way it is, you'd better stop asking for trouble,' I told him.

He was still smiling when he reached out, thrust the palm of his hand under my chin and shoved hard. It sent me staggering back a coupla paces.

It got me annoyed. If he'd tried slugging me I'd have been prepared for it. But there was something dreadfully humiliating about being shoved that way, almost as though I wasn't worth the trouble of being socked by him.

I came back quickly, wrapped my hand in his necktie and pulled it tight. 'You're gonna be sorry for that,' I said grimly.

I'd made a very big mistake when I guessed that he hadn't the guts for a rough and tumble. I guess that fella knew all there was to know about rough and tumble. Especially the dirty side of it.

The first I knew of it was when his knee came up and smashed into my groin. And instinctively, as I jack-knifed in pain, I knew what was coming next, and threw myself backwards. So instead of his fist coming up into the my puss and pulping my nose, his knuckles scraped my forehead and my scalp.

I sat down hard. But even though I was in pain, I kicked out hard at his ankles, knocking his legs beneath him so that he thudded on the ground beside me.

I reached out, hammered one hand into his guts and reached for his throat with the other. I felt his hands on my face, gouging fingers seeking for my eye sockets so he could blind me, and I began to lose my temper. I dug my thumb hard into his windpipe and jammed it deep, using all my strength. He gave a kinda gurgle and he let go of my face and grabbed my hand instead. Somehow he managed to get hold of a finger and jerked it over backwards. I coulda shrieked in agony as I felt sinews tearing and the bone arching and threatening to snap. Instinctively I lashed out with my foot and contacted his kneecap. That made him let go.

We rolled apart then, and as I scrambled to my feet, he was on his hands and knees.

But you can't start a scrap of this nature in a respectable hotel – not without somebody trying to break it up. There were a couple of guys closing in on Handsome from behind, and as I got to my feet, other hands clutched me.

Fellas can get themselves a lotta grief by sticking their noses in where they don't belong. I've found myself a lotta grief in my time for doing exactly the same kinda thing.

When those restraining hands grabbed my arms, the fellas had in mind separating a coupla guys who were scrapping and who'd probably like to be separated anyway before they hurt each other.

But I didn't wanna be separated from Handsome. He was horning in on Sally just when I was feeling in the worst mood I'd been in for months. I'd lost my girl, been sleepless all night, I'd had my pals razored up and I'd been kicked in the groin and had my finger almost broken. All those things added up. They made me fighting mad. So when those peace-loving guys started laying restraining hands on me, they soon felt sorry for it. I grabbed one pair of the hands firmly between mine, hunched my back, jerked hard and brought the fella flying over my shoulders. He landed on the ground in front of me with an awful thud. And as soon as I'd released him, I arced around with my right and clopped the other guy clean on the point.

The only other restraining hands then were those reaching out to grab Handsome, who by this time was on his feet. I made a dive at him. I slugged one of his captors hard, pulped Handsome's nose and then shouldered the other captor so hard he sat down with a thump. That quick action, working from left to right, left me and Handsome with the field to ourselves. But fast as I'd moved, I'd been just a few seconds too late. Handsome's face was dripping with blood, but he was still full of steam. The kick he started shoving out when I pulped his nose caught my thigh just on the side. It didn't hurt me much, but it spun me off my balance, and as I fell, his foot caught me again on the side of the head. Handsome wasn't kicking for fun. That kick made my head spin and my ears buzz. I climbed to my feet and climbed straight into a rip-snorter that landed under chin my slightly to the right, loosening every tooth in my jaw, snapping my head back so hard on my shoulders that it threatened to break like a twig. I guess the rest of my body musta followed my head, because I landed flat on my back, a perfect horizontal position.

Yet, three-quarters dazed as I was, the instinct of self-protection was working strong inside me. As my shoulders hit the ground, I saw Handsome, his face no longer smiling but bloody and enraged, diving at me, his fists bunched together, driving for my face. My legs seemed to work automatically, finding strength from somewhere, doubling up so that my feet took the strain against his chest and then uncoiling like a released spring. Handsome went hurtling backwards, hitting the bar with a thud that sounded like he musta broken some bones.

I got to my feet unsteadily. I stood crouched there, trying to get my breath back. Handsome was done up, too. His back musta been hurt, but he was game. He stepped in again and swung. I was watching him closely. I didn't let that swing scare me like it was intended to do. I let it whistle past my face a good six inches away and then grabbed at his foot as it came swinging towards my guts. Handsome knew a thing or two about all-in tough fighting. But I'd had my experience of that, too. I jerked hard on his foot, and as he hit the ground, I threw myself on top of him. I really got a grip on his throat this time. I dug my thumbs in deep and began to choke the life outta him. I forgot where we were, I forgot there were fellas standing around watching. I forgot everything except the mad desire to choke the life outta him. I saw his cheeks bulge and turn blue as his eyes popped and his tongue protruded. Maybe I woulda choked him to death right on the spot, because I was so made by this time that I wasn't thinking about law and order or cops or the electric chair. Looking back on it, maybe it was lucky for me there were fellas around who stuck their noses into things that didn't concern them. But it took six of them to do it. Two grabbed me by the arms, one grabbed me by the hair and jerked me backwards, and a fourth guy slugged me hard under the chin.

I'd taken a beating already. That slug under the chin hazed me up some. When I was able to sit up and take notice, there was a ring of guys standing around me. I was sitting on the floor resting my back against the wall. I began to struggle to my feet. Three or four of the guys thrust me down again.

'Take it easy, fella.'

'Where is he?'

'Take it easy. He ain't here no more.'

'I'll kill him,' I said.

One of the guys had a red swelling on his jawbone. He musta been one of the guys I'd slugged. He didn't look very pleased with me. He moved in a pace and said: 'Look, buddy. If you wanna get tough, we're all here to make it plenny tough for you.'

I said wearily, 'I ain't got no quarrel with you.'

'You're gonna take it easy?'

'Sure,' I said. 'Lemme get up and grab myself a drink.'

They watched me carefully as I scrambled to my feet. I looked around. Handsome wasn't there. Neither was Sally.

'All right, fellas,' I said. 'It's on me. What are you having?'

7

I met Jimmy and Victor at the radio station that night. Their broadcasting room wasn't a bit like I thought it would be. There were comfortable armchairs around a wide table on which rested the microphone. One wall was taken up by what looked like four gramophones standing side by side, and Jimmy had a stack of records lined up in a cabinet. Victor had a sheet of paper containing a long list of record titles.

'We're on the air in five minutes,' said Victor.

'I suppose from that time on, we don't talk.'

Victor grinned. 'Don't worry. Nothing gets broadcast unless we want.' He pointed at the mike. When I switch that on, this room is on the air. Anything we say in here can be heard on the network. But while that's switched off, nothing can be heard outside this room'

'What about the gramophone?' I asked.

'You'll see how it works,' he said. 'They're flashing red now.'

A little red light above the door began winking. Victor switched on the mike. 'Victor Lane all set to broadcast,' he said. 'Testing, testing, testing.'

'Okay,' he said a few minutes later, and switched off the mike.

'Only a minute, now,' he said.

He sat watching the clock on the wall. It had a large second hand that slowly ticked its way towards zero hour. I watched intently. Then, as the second hand hit the hour, Victor switched on the mike.

'Hello, folks,' he said in his inimitable voice. 'Here's Victor Lane joining you for another night-long session of tunes, blues and haunting melodies that'll keep you awake if you wanna go to sleep, and lull you to sleep if you wanna stay awake.'

He went on talking, wise-cracking and announcing the first record. Meanwhile, Jimmy had lined up records on the gramophones. He looked at Victor and raised his finger. Victor nodded back, and as he finished talking, Jimmy fingered a coupla switches. Victor switched off the mike and sat back in his chair. The gramophone turntable revolved soundlessly. Inside the studio, there wasn't a sound to be heard.

Victor said: 'That'll last ten minutes.'

'It is okay to talk?' I said.

'Sure.'

I looked at the gramophone. I couldn't hear a sound.

'You don't hear it in here,' explained Victor. 'The broadcast is being picked up in another room.'

'How d'you know how the record's going?' I asked.

'Same way as anybody else,' said Victor. 'I just switch on the radio like this.' He clicked a switch fastened just under the desk top, and a loudspeaker placed high up on the wall cut in with the popular strains of the record Victor had announced.

'It makes it easy for us,' explained Jimmy. 'We can take phone calls, play darts, talk, do any damn thing we please. And nothing goes out on the air until we switch on the mike. That's the only time we gotta be quiet.'

The telephone had a little bulb attached to it. The bulb began to flash noiselessly. Jimmy cradled the phone. 'Victor Lane,' he said.

The telephone voice crackled away. 'Sure,' said Jimmy. 'We can fit you up with a hot number. We ain't got 'Putting on the Ritz' in the studio, but I can put my hands on 'Ritzy Fritzy' right away.' That was one of the records he'd already got on his list.

'Sure,' Jimmy said. 'Always pleased to oblige. Gotta cut now. On the air in a few seconds.'

He hung up. 'That's the way it goes all night,' he said. 'I just have to make these fellas think I'm putting on what they want especially for them.'

The record came to an end. Victor gave us a warning glance and switched on the mike.

'D'you like that, folks? Well, maybe some of you did, maybe some of you didn't. You have to be in the mood. You have to be healthy and bright to enjoy that kinda tune.

'Are you all healthy, folks ? I knew a fella once that was awful down. It was his liver caused it. But a friend of his was a chemist and gave him a liver mixture. Boy, did that mixture put him on top of the world? I'll say it did. Listen, folks ...' Victor's voice sank to a confidential whisper ... 'D'you know, that liver mixture was so good, that two weeks after that fella died, they had to beat his liver to death with a stick.

'Well, it takes a long while to make a success of anything. But that chemist didn't take so long. That liver mixture was the real thing. He's in big business today, folks. He's sending out that liver tonic all over the world. Thousands of tins leave the factory every day. You oughta make sure you put your liver right up on top form, where it has to be if you're gonna make yourself and your family really healthy.

'Order a tin of Leyton's Liver Longer Mixture tomorrow and you'll never regret it.

'Now how about a little snort.' Victor poured water from a decanter into a glass, drank deeply and loudly and smacked his lips. 'Gee, folks,' he said in a tipsy voice, 'that wash a nicsh li'lle Schnozzle I Drant.'

Jimmy gently slid in with a record of Snozzle Durante singing his famous 'The Day I Found the Lost Chord.' Victor switched off the mike and the radio. The room seemed strangely quiet then. It was difficult to believe that fifty thousand people were listening to the gramophone playing in our room and yet we ourselves couldn't hear it.

Victor mopped his brow and sighed heavily. 'What a way to make a living,' he said.

'We all gotta eat somehow,' I said.

The telephone light began to flicker.

It went on like that, lights flickering, gramophone fading in and out, mike being switched on and off and Victor interjecting his crazy little jokes and advertisements.

Finally Victor said: 'Okay you two? After this next record.'

We waited then in a kinda pins-and-needles suspense till the record clicked off. Then Victor switched on the mike. But this time when he spoke, his voice wasn't light and gay; it was tense and serious.

'Folks, there's a kinda unpleasant subject I wanna shoot off my mouth about. Most of you folks listening now are ordinary, decent folks, doing a job of work, sending your kids to school, keeping your homes bright and clean and living like decent people should live.

'But, folks, there's nearly always one bad apple in any sack of apples. And one bad apple is liable to turn all the others rotten by contamination.

'We got our bad apple right here in this city, folks; it's a very, very rotten apple. You all know I'm talking about Ghost City, that den of vice, trafficking in dope, women and spirits and running twisted gambling games.

'I guess you all know, too, that there don't seem to be much legal activity trying to shut this place down. Seems like Ghost City is immune from the law, and has been for some years.

'That means it's up to you and me, folks. It's up to you and me to clean up this town. It's gonna be difficult. But we can make a start right now. You can all make a start by writing to the President tonight. Maybe that don't sound like a hellava thing to do. But there's fifty thousand of you listening in right now, listening at your work, in the cafés, in the garages, all kinds of places all over town. Fifty thousand letters from all you folks is gonna make quite a pile of letters. It won't wait, folks, so get out your pens or your pencils right away and get that letter in the post-box first thing in the morning. It's up to you now to start the ball rolling with a shoal of letters to the President about Ghost City.

'That's all for now, folks. There'll be more later.'

Jimmy faded in 'The Star Spangled Banner' as Victor switched off the mike.

'That'll start something,' he said.

'It has,' said Jimmy. 'That phone's been going like hell since half-way through your morality campaign. Do

I answer it?'

'I'll answer it.' Victor picked up the phone. Then he covered the mouthpiece, grinned with one eyebrow arched and said:

'It's the Police Chief. They've even cut all calls so he can get through. Listen if you can.' He pulled the earpiece away from his ear.

'Hey, Lane,' grunted a harsh voice.

'Yeah, what d'ya want?'

'Police Chief Hanagan here ...'

'I know, I know.'

'What's the meaning of putting through that broadcast?'

'Didn't take Jegger long to rope you in, did it?' said Victor.

Hanagan spluttered down the line. 'That broadcast was calculated to incite trouble,' he roared. 'Furthermore, it was a serious reflection on the official conduct of the force.'

'Is that so?' purred Victor. 'Maybe there ain't no such place as Ghost City.'

'Sure there is. But it's a respectably organised and well-run show. It's an asset to the town and draws tourists.'

'Jegger sure pays you well to blink your eyes,' said Victor.

Hanagan spluttered again. 'I'm warning you, Lane. It there's any repetition of that broadcast, we'll have you inside for contempt of public officers and for inciting civil disobedience.'

'I'd like that,' said Lane. 'Just get going. Get this case brought into court. Do it any way you like. Try getting a court order to close down the station, or smack a warrant on me. Just see how long your case will stand up in court under examination with witnesses.'

Jimmy nodded at Victor. Victor said, 'Sorry, Hanagan. On the air again.' He hung up, switched on the mike and began talking just as 'The Star Spangled Banner' finished.

'Have you heard of Nymic, folks? Have you heard of the Nymic Babies with the special, all-rubber, Nymic panties ...?'

Victor went on droning fun and advertisements into the mike. I glanced at Jimmy. He was grinning. He held up his thumbs to show he was pleased with Victor's handling of Ghost City up to date.

There were a lotta calls after that. Victor went on, talking into the mike then talking into the phone. Most of the calls were from folks who agreed with Victor's broadcast, who were writing letters to the President right away and who had their own angle on Ghost City.

The toughest call came from the owners of the radio station. Victor said he'd paid for the time he'd spent on the air, just like any other advertiser. They said to hell with that, and so on and so on. Any repetition of such a broadcast, they warned him, would constitute a breach of his contract.

Victor hung up the phone, mopped his brow and said: 'That gives us just one more chance to broadcast, anyway.'

'Then you'll be out on your neck,' I said.

'Well, I'm getting fed up with this job, anyway.'

8

We didn't have to wait long before we found out that the broadcast wasn't popular in certain circles. We found out just as soon as we quit the radio station.

We came out together, nodded at the commissionaire and pushed our way through the swing doors. I was the first outside, and as I took a deep breath of the fresh morning air and looked across the pavement toward the café, a car that was parked a hundred yards along the road started up and drove down towards us.

I turned quickly, spread my arms to stop Victor and Jimmy, and rapped: 'Get back inside, quickly.'

'What the …?' began Victor.

I didn't argue. I thrust hard at both of them, and some of my urgency got over to them. They turned and stumbled back through the swing doors, with me pushing hard behind them. I could hear the roar of the car as it leaped towards us, and was conscious that the top half of the swing doors was of glass.

'Get down,' I yelled, and threw myself forward, half-tackling Victor and Jimmy, sprawling them and myself on the ground as the rattle of a machine-gun drowned the roar of the car engine. Glass splintered and showered down on top of us and wooden splinters flew around as the doors jumped and split beneath the impact of the lead.

It seemed strangely quiet when the roar of the car died in the distance and the rattle of machine-gun fire had ceased. There was a haze of dust as I scrambled to my feet, cutting my hand on a glass splinter as I did so. My cheek smarted, and when I put my hand there I found a splinter of wood sticking into my cheek like a dart.

Jimmy and Victor were both okay. All of us were covered in glass splinters and had minor little cuts, but there was nothing that amounted to anything.

'Nice boys to play with,' said Victor. He took off his coat and shook it. You don't brush glass splinters from your clothes with your hands.

The commissionaire appeared. He was white-faced, trembling slightly. He just gaped at the splintered, lead-torn doors.

'Get the cops on the phone,' Jimmy told him. 'Tell them there's been a shooting. Nobody hurt,' he added.

The commissionaire nodded dumbly, looked with awe again at the door and ambled off to the phone.

'What d'ya think the cops will do?' said Victor.

'Maybe nothing,' said Jimmy. 'But the proper thing is to report.'

'Sure, sure. Let's be legal about everything we do.'

'Have you booked for breakfast across the road?' I said.

'Always go there,' said Victor.

'Maybe it'll be a good plan to vary habit, today,' I suggested. 'We may have a very special dish served up if we go there. Let's go back to your flat instead.'

Victor arched his eyebrows. 'Maybe you got

something there,' he agreed.

I cautiously poked my head outta the door. It seemed clear enough outside. After a time, I flagged a taxi that was crawling past outside and we climbed aboard.

At Victor's flat, we rustled together a breakfast, talked for a while and then grabbed ourselves some shut-eye. It was tiring work being on all night.

The next move from Ghost City came during the late afternoon. We'd had a lunch sent up from the around the corner and had played backgammon for a time when the bell to the flat buzzed. I looked at Victor, he looked at me. Then he went over to a sideboard, opened a drawer and took out a small automatic, which he thrust in his pocket.

All three of us went to the door. The bell sounded again. Victor motioned to us to stand either side of the door and then yelled, 'Who is it?'

There was silence for a moment, then: 'A coupla guys that wanna talk to you, Lane.'

Victor said: 'You can come in. But there's a coupla guns gonna be trained on you all the time. How does that sound?'

'That sounds fine. We ain't starting anything.'

Victor raised his eyebrows at me questioningly. 'Shall we let 'em in?'

'They'll poke a tommy in your belly, pull the trigger and scram.'

Victor said loudly, 'Hey, you fellas, there's one more thing. Just in case you've any fancy ideas, I'm carrying a coupla pineapples. If you wanna talk peaceably, that's okay by me. But if you got any ideas about slinging lead, maybe you'll get me first. But these pineapples will get you just the same when I hit the floor.'

'Quit playing, Lane,' drawled the fella outside. 'We wanna talk. We ain't even rodded up.'

Victor took a deep breath, put one hand in his pocket where he held the automatic and swung the door wide.

The two fellas standing outside were the two plug-uglies who'd carved up Victor in the café. They stood there, their hands well clear of their pockets as though to show they intended no harm.

I could see the hairs bristle on the nape of Victor's neck as he looked at the tall fella. There was a sticking plaster on Victor's face, and beneath it a nasty gash that would scar him for life. The tall guy had caused it.

Victor said: 'Ah, now this is a real pleasure. Just come in, will you?'

The tall guy looked slightly uneasy. Squatty grinned. 'Surprised to see us? 'he asked.

'On the contrary, I'm delighted,' said Victor. He stepped back a pace. 'One at a time, please,' he said.

Squatty came in first. He dropped his eyes to the level of Victor's pocket, showing he knew there was a gun in that pocket, and a slight grin curled around his lips. Without being asked, he raised his hands above his head and turned around. I ran my fingers over him from top to bottom, even feeling along his legs and arms. He wasn't carrying any weapon. Neither was the tall guy. I was especially on the look-out for any kind of a razor.

They preceded us through into the living room, picked the most comfortable chairs and sprawled out comfortably.

'Well,' said Victor grimly. He still had his hand in his pocket.

'Nice place you got here,' said Squatty, looking

around. 'Wouldn't have a drink in it, by any chance?'

'Feel thirsty?' asked Victor.

'Just a bit.'

'Got thirsty driving around the streets with a machine-gun on your lap, I suppose,' said Victor.

'You mean the shoot-up at the radio station?'

'What else?'

Squatty fished a pack of cigarettes from his pocket and lit up without offering anyone else a cigarette. 'You got us boys wrong, fella. We don't operate like that.'

'You just use your feet and razors?' asked Victor.

Squatty shrugged. 'You know how it is. You got a job to do, well you just do it.'

Victor said slowly and deliberately, 'Well, before I start to beat the living daylights outta you two guys, maybe you'd like to say what's on your mind.'

Squatty screwed up one eye in a wink. 'You ain't gonna start getting tough, pal.'

'No?'

'Naw.' Squatty shook his head and scattered ash on the carpet. 'You're a regular kinda guy, and you ain't gonna be the kinda guy that gets unfair.'

'Meaning what?'

'Meaning that we've come here under a kinda white flag. It's a kinda truce.'

I walked over to Squatty, slapped the cigarette from his hand and smacked him hard across the face. The tall guy watched me impassively. Squatty nestled further into the chair. His cheek was stinging from the blow I'd given him and his eyes glared balefully. But all he did was to say: 'I didn't have to come here, fella. I came here for your own good as much as anything.'

Victor said: 'Leave him alone, Hank. Let him do the talking first and leave the rough stuff to me later.'

Squatty said: 'You three guys can earn yourselves five grand apiece, right now. Just imagine. I came all the way here to tell you that, and you wanna start getting tough about it.'

Victor said: 'Spit it out. What's the game?'

'Do I have to draw a map?' asked Squatty. 'There's five grand each for you if you'll pack your bags and git outta town tonight.'

'And if we don't take the five grand? '

Squatty shrugged. 'I don't know. I ain't got any instructions about that.'

'Who's employing you?'

Squatty grinned. 'That'd be telling.'

'It's Jegger who's employing you, isn't it? '

Squatty ignored the question. 'How about it, fellas? You want the five grand?'

Victor said: 'You can go back and tell Jegger we'll see him and Ghost City in flames before we're through. And he can use his five grand to paper the wall of his toilet, which is about all his money is good for.'

Squatty got up slowly. He said: 'I'm kinda sorry you guys ain't taking the easy way out of this.'

Victor said: 'Just a minute, you and me have got something to talk over.' He gave Squatty a thrust so he flopped back in his chair.

'I've got a cut on this cheek that's gotta be paid for,' said Victor. 'Which of you guys is gonna be first?'

Squatty said: 'There's a law against beating up innocent citizens. You don't wanna find yourself charged with assault and battery, do you?'

'That makes me laugh,' said Victor. 'Now, make up your mind, which one first? Or both together if you like.'

Squatty shrugged his shoulders, pursed his lips and gave a loud, piercing whistle.

Immediately there came a hammering on the door of the flat. 'Open up,' yelled a deep voice. 'Open up, there.'

'Who the hell's that?' I asked.

Squatty grinned. 'That's the cops, I guess. They have to stick around sometimes to make sure there's no breach of the peace.'

The hammering on the door increased in sound and weight. 'Open up. Open up in the name of the law.'

Victor said: 'Better open up, Jimmy, or they'll break the door down.' Then, as Jimmy went off, he looked at Squatty. 'Sometime,' he promised, 'we're gonna meet up some place where you ain't gonna have the bribed law hanging just around the corner. When that time comes, you two heels are gonna find out how much interest I'm willing to pay for this.' He fingered his cheek.

Jimmy came back. There were a coupla cops trailing behind him. The first cop said to Squatty, 'What's the trouble here?'

'No trouble,' said Squatty. 'We're just leaving.'

He and the tall guy got up. They walked to the door, and the cops followed behind them. We stood there impotently, wanting like hell to start something but knowing how crazy it would be to run foul of the cops when they'd just like to have an excuse to shove us in the cooler to stop the scandal about Ghost City.

When the door dosed behind them, Victor stood and swore loud and long.

'One thing,' I said when he'd finished. 'We're getting Jegger worried good and proper.'

Jimmy was standing over by the window. He said: 'Look at this.' Me and Victor joined him window. Downstairs, a cream, open tourer-type auto was parked on the opposite side of the road. Squatty and the tall guy were climbing into it. A third man was sitting behind the steering column.

'So they're mixed up with Foster,' breathed Jimmy.

'Yeah,' I said. 'And what does Foster do?'

'He's the agent for Ghost City. He's reckoned to handle the women and dope supplies.'

'Is that so,' I breathed, and my heart went pit-pat, because I recognised Foster. He was Sally's friend, Handsome.

9

I'd been all mixed up inside about Sally until I'd had the trouble with Handsome. After that, I'd thought things over and seen them differently. Sally was right, of course. We'd been good pals, but we weren't cut out to spend the rest of our lives in harness. All those little quarrels and bickers we'd had were the result of strained nerves. And our nerves were strained because we'd been trying to make something very special when we hadn't the right material. We'd been both trying to make ourselves believe we were a match for life when the most we could be was good pals.

It was inevitable we should break up the way we had. Sally had realised this more clearly than I had realised it. But where Sally was wrong was in not being prepared for us to continue as good pals. All right, I agreed with her, we weren't a match. But she didn't have to treat me as though I was a leper and as though she daren't speak to me for fear of contamination.

It was this attitude of hers that rankled and hurt. I wasn't hurt because things hadn't worked out between us. I was just hurt because she no longer regarded me as a friend.

But even so, as soon as I learned that Handsome was Foster, and that Foster was tied up with Ghost City and the agent for dope and dames, I got worried about Sally.

Maybe she had handed me the frozen mitt. Maybe she'd rather have Foster's company than speak a civil word to me. But that didn't alter the fact that I still regarded her as my friend. And I knew enough of Sally to know that she wouldn't push around with Foster if she knew what he did for a living.

What was more to the point was just how dangerous Foster might be to Sally.

I said to Victor: 'Look, you two. I gotta little business I wanna contract. I'll meet you two fellas over at the radio station tonight.'

Victor said, 'Better watch your step, Hank. Those two guys mean trouble.'

'I've met trouble before. And I've got even bigger troubles on my mind now.'

'Okay. As you wish.' Victor shrugged his shoulders.

I went over to the door. As I opened it, Victor said: 'I'm gonna blow everything on the air tonight. It'll be my last chance. Maybe it'll be our last chance. You don't have to be in on this, Hank. You can keep out. I can handle it alone.'

'How you rate yourself,' I mocked. 'Always out to get all the glory yourself. Well, it ain't gonna work, Victor. I'm gonna be right there with you. When the medals are handed out, I'll be right up there with you, waiting to get mine as well.'

He grinned. 'I'm gonna welcome company. If somebody starts slinging out lead, we'll divide it between the three of us.'

'I'll be there,' I promised.

I went straight back to the hotel. There was just one thing I wanted to do. And that was to get hold of Sally, make her listen to me and make her understand just what kind of a fella Foster really was.

I went over to the reception clerk as soon as I got in the hotel. He looked at me apprehensively. He'd been there when I'd had the fight with Foster in the bar. He'd got the feeling I was a tough guy and should be treated with respect.

I asked him to connect me by phone to Sally's room. I reasoned I had much more chance to speak to her first on the phone than by just barging into her room. The way she was feeling now, she'd probably start ringing for the house dick as soon as she saw me.

The reception clerk said: 'She's gone out. Went out lunch time and hasn't been back.'

'How can you be so damn sure?' I growled.

He explained. 'I've been on duty all the time. I saw her go out, and she left her key here. The key's still here. You can see it.'

I glanced at the key rack. Sure enough, the key of her room was on the hook.

I frowned at him. 'Was she alone?'

He said nervously, 'Now look, mister. You ain't gonna start no more trouble in this hotel, are you?'

I guessed what he was getting at. I said: 'So she's gone out with Foster?'

'I didn't say so,' he protested. But he didn't say it like he meant it.

'Five bucks argues you know where they went,' I said.

'Five bucks is a good argument. But it don't win the prize, because I ain't got the prize to give away.'

I tried wheedling. 'Look, you've been around here a while. When a dame and a fella go out after lunch, what kinda place would they go?'

He shrugged. 'This is a big city, mister. Maybe they went swimming, coulda gone dancing. There's plenty of cinemas in this town, and it's a nice drive out to the Indian reservation. I guess two folks like you mention could go almost anywhere.'

I turned away from the desk with a grunt. The fella was right. It was a big city and two people could go almost any place. But that didn't mean to say I wasn't gonna try finding them.

I spent a coupla hours running around town. I went to cafés and I went in bars. I drank a lotta coffee and a lotta rye and I saw a lotta people. But I didn't see the two people I was looking for.

I went back to the hotel. The same reception clerk was there.

I said: 'Is she back yet?'

He shook his head. But he was tensed up as though he knew something and wasn't sure if he should tell me about it.

I helped him out: 'Anything happen I'd be interested in?'

He looked at me and then he looked around to make sure there was nobody within earshot. He said: 'Have you still got five bucks that can put up an argument?'

I pulled a five-dollar bill from my pocket and slid it under the blotter on his desk.

He said: 'Maybe what I've got ain't what you want. I still don't know where she is.'

'There's five dollars there. Make the story good, willya?'

He glanced around him again, moistened his lips and then leaned forward across the counter.

'That fella Foster came back,' he said.

I tensed all over. He musta seen that. He said quickly, 'He ain't here now. He's gone again.' He was holding something back in the way a miser holds on to his dough.

'What did he want?' I growled.

'Foster settled her bill for her,' he said. 'He paid up and checked out for her. How am I doing?'

'You're doing swell,' I said. Inside, I was tensed like a coiled spring. 'What next?'

'It rates five dollars?' he said.

'Sure.'

He picked up the five spot and folded it into a neat little wad. 'Foster took all her luggage with him.'

I eyed him carefully. 'Is that all?'

'Sure, mister, that's all.'

'Didn't you find out where he was going?'

'Sure I tried. But he wouldn't talk. Just paid the bill. Said she was waiting for him.'

I looked at my watch. It was seven-thirty. Victor went on the air at midnight. That gave me about four and a half hours to find Sally before things really broke. After Victor got through denouncing Ghost City, things might get so hot for him, Jimmy Chark and me that there might be no more time to look for Sally.

I didn't know how, where or when to look for Foster and Sally. I hadn't a single lead to work on. But I just went out of that hotel with one idea in my mind; to find Sally at all costs. I was the only friend Sally had in town, and I just simply had to get her out of Foster's influence as soon as I could.

I went on looking.

I was still looking at a quarter to eleven. I was still looking at a quarter to twelve. I knew I should be at the radio station to meet Victor, but reckoned he'd give me an hour's grace.

At a quarter past twelve, tired and worn out with worry, I stuck my head inside just one more drug store. It was almost empty and I could see at a glance that Sally wasn't there. I turned to go out and suddenly remembered I hadn't eaten since late afternoon.

I went over to the counter and sat up on a stool. I ordered coffee and sandwiches. I was on the point of giving up now. For all I knew, Sally and Foster could have beaten it right out of town. The radio was playing. It was one of Strauss's waltzes. And when the record finished, Victor's familiar voice came on the air.

But there was a difference about his voice. The same difference that there had been when he'd attacked Ghost City the previous night. I tensed and waited.

Sure enough, Victor was attacking again. But this was really the works. He attacked with everything he had. He blew the top off Ghost City with everything he knew. Jegger, the cops, Foster, and even the two razor-men came in for his attack.

There were only a few guys in that drug store, but what Victor said and the way he said it got them right off their seats. I glanced around at their faces. They were listening intently, every face registering strong feeling.

And then it suddenly came home to me. Here was I, sitting in this drug store listening to Victor put it over. There might be trouble any time, and I wasn't there to give Victor a hand.

I had to put Sally on one side then. I'd done my best for her, but something more urgent had arisen now. Still biting at my hamburger, I made for the door. I'd got my car outside. I climbed in, gunned the engine and got going.

It musta taken me twenty minutes to get to the radio station, and all the time I was expecting to see it shot to pieces, blown to pieces, maybe even in flames.

But as I drew up outside, everything seemed peaceful.

I slammed outta the car, ran up the steps, pushed through the newly-repaired swing doors and ran right into Victor's arms.

'Jeesus,' I said. 'Why the hell didn't you wait for me before you started?'

He grinned. 'Lots of reasons. Got your car?'

'Sure, it's outside. But what reasons?'

'I'll tell you on the way back to my flat.'

'But what about the broadcast?'

He grinned. 'Finished,' he said. 'Contract torn up. You should have heard that telephone when I got broadcasting.'

As he talked, we'd been walking out and down the steps to my car. Some sixth sense operated, and as I caught a glimpse of a dark shadow moving towards us from the side, I flung myself in that direction, cannoned into somebody and instinctively and defensively clutched at his arms.

Victor was right behind me. He had his fist drawn back, ready to slam it hard in the fella's face, when he stopped suddenly. Then his arm dropped to his side. 'Okay, Hank,' he said. 'It's Phillip. He's a friend of Jimmy's.'

I let the fella go. He was slight of build, toothy and quite brown-skinned. He said: 'I've gotta see you. It's pretty important. It's about Jimmy.'

I felt Victor stiffen. 'Yeah?' he demanded.

I was acutely conscious that anything might blow up any time now, and we were all sitting birds, outlined on the steps in front of the radio station.

'Let's get going,' I said. 'We can talk later.'

Victor and Phillip climbed into the back of the car.

'I'll make for your flat,' I said.

Phillip interrupted. He said, 'No. You'll go to Mason Avenue.'

I got sarcastic. 'I'm at your service, sir.'

But Victor's voice was serious. 'Do what he says, Hank. We can trust him.'

What Victor said was okay by me. I turned the car around.

Phillip said: 'Jimmy was hurt bad. I was with him.' He pulled up the sleeve of his jacket. I glanced over my shoulder. He was wearing a white bandage that stretched from elbow to wrist. The bandage was stained red.

Victor said grimly: 'How bad is Jimmy?'

Phillip said: 'Jimmy's hurt bad. But he's very strong. There were people around when we were attacked and they came to help. Afterwards, I took Jimmy to my home. He wanted to come to you at the radio station. But I wouldn't let him. I said he must rest. And then I promised to bring you to him.'

'You're a good friend,' said Victor. 'Better step it up a bit, Hank,' he added.

As we drove, Victor explained why he had made the broadcast early. Neither Jimmy Chark nor I had arrived on time. He didn't say this, but it may have been in his mind that we were both scared. But it suddenly occurred to Victor that if he put over the broadcast right away, the chances were that any tough business Jegger started would be in the early morning, just at the time when Victor usually left the radio station.

But if he made his broadcast early, put on a series of records with the automatic record-changer working and just walked out of the station, Jegger wouldn't have time to start reprisals.

And that's just what Victor did.

By the time he'd finished explaining this, we'd arrived at Phillip's place. We climbed outta the car, followed Phillip up stone steps to the front door and then up two flights of stairs to his apartment.

When we got inside, Jimmy was sitting in a chair wearing only his trousers. It didn't look like Jimmy at first, because his face was so swollen and bruised and there was a piece of sticking plaster stretched across his forehead.

There were two long gashes on his chest, each about six inches long. The skin at the edges of the cuts had shrunk back so that they looked like open mouths. Jimmy was carefully cleansing the cuts with antiseptic. He must have been suffering intense agony, but as we came in, he looked up and grinned. There must have been quite a lot of his forefathers' blood passed down to him. Only an Indian could have borne such pain so stoically.

Victor said: 'So they got you. I told you not to chase off that way.'

Jimmy said: 'They got me. But I'm glad I went. I found out all I need to know, now.'

'It musta been good if you're willing to pay this much,' said Victor. He went close and looked Jimmy over. He hadn't only been cut about, he'd been banged about. His body was covered with angry blue welts. His back was welted from neck to waist.

'Rubber hose with a lead core,' explained Jimmy

simply. 'If Phillip here hadn't yelled long enough for folk to take an interest, they might have finished me.'

'Squatty and the tall guy?' guessed Victor.

Jimmy nodded. And then, as though dismissing the question of his injuries as unimportant, he said: 'I know all about Jegger now, Victor. He's rotten, just the way you said. I'm not arguing for him anymore. In fact … well, that's my business.'

'Jegger is the business of all of us,' said Victor grimly.

'Mine especially,' said Jimmy.

'Jegger suddenly bitten you or something?'

Jimmy looked at Phillip. 'You tell them,' he said.

Phillip said: 'There ain't much to tell. But you've probably heard that during the last coupla years there's been trouble up at the reservation from time to time.'

'I heard,' said Victor. 'They smuggled whisky in somehow.'

'That's it,' said Phillip. 'Well, last week, Jimmy got me to go up to the reservation and look around. Nothing in particular, but just to keep an eye on things. Well, I found out about that whisky.'

'Jegger?' guessed Victor.

Phillip nodded. 'That's it. He's been putting on the act of being the good Samaritan, sending up food and books and teachers for the benefit of the reservation. But that was just a cover. He's been smuggling up whisky every time he took a load of food. The so-called teachers are just there to keep control over the whisky and where it's cached, and to ration it out. And every time a load of whisky is shifted up there, Jegger comes back with load of skins worth probably fifty or sixty times as much as the whisky cost him.'

'You've just found this out?'

'Found it out tonight and came back to tell Jimmy. There's a kind of ceremonial pow-wow up on the reservation tonight. Jegger's been invited along as the guest of honour. He's up there now. He's got a van there loaded with skins. He'd never get out if the cops did their job. But they must be in this with him.'

Jimmy said grimly, 'That's what he's doing to my people.'

Victor said: 'Your people ain't specially privileged. There's Ghost City to take care of the palefaces, remember?'

I suddenly remembered about Sally. I said: 'Jimmy, you knew this Foster fella. What's he likely to do with a girl?'

Jimmy shot me a strange glance. 'Do you know any girl that's going around with him?'

'Sure,' I said. 'A friend of mine.'

'Get her away from him quick,' he advised.

'Yeah, that's what I reckoned to do. But he's checked out of her hotel for her. They've gone off together.'

Jimmy said: 'Foster's a quick worker. Have you looked around Ghost City?'

'That's crazy,' I said. 'She ain't the kinda girl to go to Ghost City. In fact, I know from experience that she dislikes the place.'

'That doesn't mean a thing,' said Jimmy.

I stared at him. Victor said softly, 'What Jimmy means, Hank, is that dames might not want to go there, but they arrive there just the same. That's the way it works.'

I took a deep breath as it suddenly came home to me that I'd been wasting precious time when I might have taking Ghost City apart looking for Sally. I made for the door.

Victor grabbed me roughly by the arm. 'Where are you going, you fool?'

I shook my arm free. 'Where d'you think?'

Victor arched his eyebrow. 'Do you realise that Jegger's crowd is going to be looking all over town for us three before long? Maybe they're even doing it now.'

I said: 'There's a dame been taken down to Ghost City. She's a nice, clean kid. What would you do?'

Victor's eyebrow arched even higher. He said slowly, 'I guess I'd do just what you're gonna do, Hank. I'd walk right into the spider's parlour.'

'All right, then.' I walked over to the door.

'But I'd do something else,' said Victor. 'I'd ask my pals to come along too.'

I looked at him steadily. 'You've got enough grief,' I said.

'I like it. I lap it up. I wouldn't miss this for anything.'

'Okay,' I said. 'Maybe it'll teach you better sense in future.'

It was Victor who took the lead, ran down the steps and climbed into my car. It was almost as though Sally was his worry and I was stringing along with him. He even drove my car.

'Pity Jimmy was in no shape to come,' he commented as we got near Ghost City.

'Perhaps it's just as well for his health,' I said drily.

10

When we arrived at Ghost City, we parked the car and went through the main street. Although it musta been well after midnight, Ghost City was fully alive as though it was only just waking up. It was much about the same as it had been when I'd gone there previously. Apart from the city guys and their dames, dressed in city clothes, you'd have thought you'd stepped straight into a Western town back in the eighteen-sixties.

Victor said: 'There really ain't much chance anybody here is gonna jump us. They're all employees, doing a job. They don't have to worry about Jegger running his business.'

It looked that way, too. The fellas that ran Ghost City lived there, worked there and played there. They fleeced the tourists and got a percentage of the takings between them. It was just a job to them, and the tourists didn't mind being fleeced just a bit either. Where else in the world could you step back in the past by a hundred years? The novelty was worth the fleecing.

Victor said: 'It's no use bothering with this part of the town.' He was referring to the part of the town we were walking through. It was the part I'd already visited.

Tinny pianos tinkled from saloons, city folk sat at tables on the sidewalks and ate dinner, an occasional cowboy galloped along the dusty street loosing off blank shots from a big revolver.

'This way,' said Victor. He turned off along a small gully between two saloons. He seemed to know his way, and I strung along with him. At the end of the gully, we came to a fence. On the other side of it, leaning with his arms on the top rail, was a tough-looking Westerner. He was talking to a city guy and his dame. As we came up, he said to the man:

'Look, stranger, thyar's plenny doin' in the town. Yuh doan't wanna come past hyar.'

The man said: 'What's special about this part, anyway? I'll pay. My money's good.'

The Westerner chewed for several seconds and then spat into the dust. He rolled his eyes towards the girl.

'Sorry, fella,' he said. 'Wimmin ain't allowed in this'n part of the town.'

'But she's with me. She came here with me.'

The Westerner chewed some more. 'Look, son,' he said. 'Yuh got yuhrself a womin. Ef yuh ain't got a womin, now, then mebbe it'd be worth yuh while comin' hyar. It's fur men only, son.'

The city fella looked like he was going to argue more. He wasn't very smart on the uptake. But the dame realised what was meant. She tugged him by the arm. 'Come on, Gail. I guess I don't want to go here, anyway. Let's go home.'

She pulled Gail away, and as the Westerner look us, Victor fumbled in his pocket.

'Five dollars apiece,' said the Westerner laconically.

Victor raised his eyebrows at the price. But he didn't argue. He handed over the notes, and the Westerner stood on one side so we could duck through under the wooden cross-bars.

There were three main streets leading off from the point of entry. Outside, they looked pretty much like the part of the town we'd just left: saloons, eathouses and dance-bars, mostly two-storey buildings.

Victor said: 'You take this street to the right, I'll take this one to the left. When you get through, meet me back here and we'll take the centre street together. If Foster brought Sally here, she'll be in one of these places somewhere.'

We split up then. The first place I came to was a big saloon. I pushed inside and looked around. It was pretty crowded. Plenty of city fellas, mostly middle-aged businessmen, seemed to find their way to this part of Ghost City. The Westeners, of course, were so serving and lounging around in their fancy Western clothes. A Western trio were hitting up an old Western melody with an accordion, a banjo and a fiddle.

But there was a new element in this part of the town that wasn't in the other part. This element was the dames. They were dressed Western fashion, too, but rather along the lines that you'd see them dressed for a vaudeville show.

The dames were all dressed the same way. The wore white, sleeveless blouses buttoned low in the front. Around their wrists they had black, patent leather guards spangled with sequins, and they wore short, brown suede cowgirl skirts fringed at the bottom. Those skirts were really short! The bottom of the skirt was about six inches above their knees, and the split up the side of the skirt didn't finish until it reached the top.

Judging from what the split showed, it looked like those girls couldn't have been wearing a thing underneath those skirts except maybe a g-string.

Additional trappings to give the Western effect were brightly-coloured 'kerchiefs knotted loosely around their necks and white Stetsons balanced at an angle over their curls.

Maybe they should have been wearing black patent riding boots, too – that would have increased the Western effect. But they weren't. They were wearing black patent, very high-heeled shoes, which, coupled with the short skirts, made their bare legs seem long and slender. The Western effect wasn't the only effect the proprietors of the joint wanted to get over!

I wasn't expecting anything quite like this, and I stood there for a moment, looking around. The girls were sitting at tables with the city men, laughing and drinking. Some were dancing. The dancing couples looked like they were going into clinches rather than dancing. And the place was jam-full. There wasn't even room up by the bar.

Just to one side was a flight of wooden steps leading upstairs. I couldn't see what was beyond the top of the stairs. But since I was sure Sally wasn't on the ground floor, I decided to have a look around up there.

A burly Westerner lazily blocked my way as I got to the foot of the staircase.

'Sorry, pard. Yuh can't go up thyar unless yuh got yuhself a womin.'

I looked at him and debated whether or not I should slug him. Then I glanced around. There were other Westerners idling at the bar. Two of them were watching. It was obvious that from time to time they encountered trouble and they were ready to deal with it.

I said, 'Okay. Where can I get a dame?'

He stroked his chin. 'Waal, we're pretty busy, pard. Guess you'll just have to wait yuh turn.'

I went over to the bar, ordered myself a drink and looked around. Those cowgirls sure were in demand. There wasn't one that didn't seem to have at least a coupla guys buying her drinks. That, of course, was part of her use, to get the customers to buy drinks. And the prices of the drinks were way up in the sky.

A few minutes later, I saw a cowgirl and a fella coming down the stairs. I walked over quickly and heard the girl plead with the fella: 'Just one drink, huh?'

'Nuthin' doin',' he said. 'I told ya. I gotta go.'

He shook off her detaining arm and out hurriedly, just as though he might have a wife waiting for him somewhere.

I took the girl by the arm. 'Okay,' I said, 'Let's go.'

She looked at me with hard eyes, but deep down I could read a kinda weariness. There were tiny lines at the corners of her eyes, and beneath her make-up her face looked a deadly white.

She took me by the arm and pushed me towards a table. 'Let's have a drink first.'

I said, 'Nix on the drink. I wanna go upstairs.'

'Have a drink first,' she insisted.

I took her by the arm roughly. 'Upstairs, that's where I wanna go, and now.'

This time there was entreaty in her eyes, 'Jeezus, gimme a break willya, fella. Lemme sit down for an hour and rest, willya. I won't drink anything expensive.'

I said grimly: 'I'll give you a break when we get upstairs.'

She flashed me a look of hatred. 'Go get yourself some other dame.'

I didn't intend spending my time hanging around that joint all night. I said: 'Are you coming upstairs or am I gonna put in a squawk that you won't play?'

That got her scared. But it didn't make her like me.

'Got a hundred bucks?'

That sure was high. I said: 'Are you dames supposed to be wrapped in gold leaf? '

She said bitterly, 'You'd think I was giving myself away if you knew the percentage I get after overhead deductions have been made.'

She led the way over to the stairs. The Westerner there held out his hand. 'It's a hundred bucks, fella.'

I paid over the dough and he stuffed it into a metal box screwed on the wall. The girl said: 'Don't forget to book it.'

The Westerner grunted and put a tick on a kinda score sheet.

'Pretty busy?' I asked as we climbed the stairs.

She glared at me malevolently. 'Just like I said, fella. You're gonna wish you hadn't paid that hundred bucks.'

She led the way along a corridor, past other doors, until she got to number nine. She opened the door and went inside. I followed her.

She took off her hat and wearily began to unbutton the front of her blouse.

'You got a toilet here?' I asked.

'Down the end of the corridor.'

'I'll be back,' I told her.

I went outside into the corridor. There was only one way to find out if Sally was around, and that was by looking in each room. And that's just what I did. I looked in every room, and there wasn't one room that wasn't occupied, and there was something going on in every room. Some fellas just gaped at me when I opened the door and nosed. Others swore viciously and bawled me out. It made me hot under the collar doing all that rubber-necking. But when I got through, I knew Sally wasn't in that building.

I went back into the girl's room and she was in bed, glaring at me across the top of the sheet.

I said, 'You wanted a break, sister. Well, you can have it. Get dressed. We're going down.'

She gaped at me.

'Jeezus,' I said. 'Are you deaf or something?'

I lit a cigarette and glanced though the window at the dusty street beneath while she dressed. It didn't take her long, because she hadn't all that much to put on. There was respect in her voice when she said: 'Okay, mister.'

I turned around and opened the door. She took my arm as we walked down the stairs. 'Gee, mister, I'm sure grateful. We've been so busy today, I feel a hundred years old.'

'You know what you're doing,' I warned her. 'In a coupla years' time, you'll feel a thousand years old.'

The next two places along the street were single-storied necking houses catering for public necking and a special kinda floor show.

The third place was just a drinking saloon. There were no dames at all in the place. It was strictly men only, and I only poked my nose inside and then ducked out again quickly. At least the other places were natural!

The next joint was a two-storied place with large windows.

There was a cowgirl standing in the entrance, leaning provocatively against the door post. She was more provocative than the others I'd seen, because she wasn't wearing a blouse. She was just wearing the coloured 'kerchief around her neck.

I'd almost reached the door when a second cowgirl escorted a city man to the door. He said goodnight and brushed past me. The second girl was a blonde, and she too had discarded her blouse. Both girls looked at me and smiled winningly.

'How about coming in for a drink, fella?'

I looked at Blondie and my heart gave a kinda jump.

I said, 'Don't mind if I do,' and I could hear my heart pounding away with excitement so loudly I was afraid they'd hear it.

I followed them inside, and there was a third girl gently rocking herself backwards and forwards in a rocking chair. She was very dark, very pretty and fascinating. Like the other two, she wasn't wearing a blouse, and unlike the other two, she wasn't even wearing a 'kerchief around her neck.

She smiled as she caught my eyes on her. 'Nice, huh?' she asked.

'Yeah. Kinda pleasing.'

'That's what we aim to be.'

Blondie had set some glasses on a table and was pouring from a bottle of rye. I glanced around quickly. There was a flight of stairs leading upwards to a kinda balcony, and I could see the doors of two rooms.

The furnishing of the downstairs room was Western style, with lariats, riding whips, horseshoes and pelts pinned around the log-wood walls.

The girl without a 'kerchief said: 'What's your name?'

'Hank,' I told her, still looking around. There didn't seem to be any male guardians in this joint.

'I'm called Helga,' she said. She pointed at the other dark girl. 'She's Suzy.' She pointed at Blondie. 'And she's called Fairy.'

'Pleased to meecher,' I said , drily. The front windows were the only windows in the place. I said: 'I'm bashful. Mind if I pull the curtains?'

'Help yourself, honey,' said Helga. She was rocking herself backwards and forwards slowly.

I pulled the curtains on both windows, went to the door and turned the key in the lock.

Blondie paused in the act of pouring. Her look hardened to one of suspicion. I dropped the key in my pocket and said with a laugh, 'I'm kinda bashful. And I'm kinda jealous. Guess I like to feel I've got you three babies to myself. I've got the dough for it, too.'

Then the tension eased. Blondie asked: 'Do you want yours straight or with soda?'

'Straight,' I said. Suzy pulled a chair up to the table for me, and Blondie sat on the table. She sat on the table in such a way, with one leg on and one leg off, that her thigh came out through her split skirt. I could see her leg from ankle to hip, and she knew I could see it.

I was still standing, and Blondie lifted her glass to her lips, giving me a silent toast. Her eyes smiled at me wickedly across the top of the glass.

'You three dames run this joint alone?' I asked casually.

Suzy chuckled. She had a husky voice. 'You couldn't imagine it being run by men, could you? Say, fella, you ain't drinking.'

As she spoke, she crossed her legs. When she did it, she knew what she was doing. At the same time, she toyed with her 'kerchief. It hadn't been much use as a covering the way it had been before. When she'd got the 'kerchief slung around and hanging down over her shoulders, it wasn't no covering at all.

I began to sweat. My shirt was sticking to my shoulders and the palms of my hands were sticky. These three dames were real hot stuff. They looked good, and they knew how to make themselves look even better. For a moment, I almost wished that I was there without any business on hand .. until I remembered what kinda dames these three girls were.

I looked at Blondie and said grimly, 'Blondie, you're on the spot.'

She stared at me.

I said: 'You and me are gonna have a little talking to do, sister. And if I don't get the right answers, I'm gonna get tough.'

They were startled. They sat up, suddenly alert.

Blondie said quietly, 'Scram, Helga.'

Helga came out of her chair like a shot from a gun. She made a dash towards the rear of the room. Even as she began to move, I knew what she was after. There was another door there, one that wouldn't be locked. She was going to get help.

I'd anticipated that move. But even so, Helga moved so quickly, she almost made it. I moved at the same time as she did, and grabbed at her. All I got was a handful of skirt. Helga went on running and left the skirt in my hands. I ploughed right on after her, reached her just as she got her hand on the door knob, grasped her by the shoulders, swung her around and sent her sprawling into the centre of the room.

None of them moved as I locked that door and dropped the key in my pocket. They just eyed me steadily, but there was a disconcerting confidence in their bearing. They didn't look scared like they should have done.

Helga clambered to her feet. I'd been right about what those dames could wear under those skirts. All Helga was wearing was a suede g-string supported a thin leather thong, slung low-down around her loins.

Blondie said slowly: 'Look, fella. You got the wrong number. We ain't no sob sisters. If you want trouble, we can hand it out. We can look after ourselves, and you ain't the first tough guy that wanted to play rough. Now, if you're smart, you can clear out right now. You ain't caused much trouble yet, and we'll forget about everything. How about it?'

They were just three dames, and they weren't gonna stop me. I was after finding Sally, and even if they'd been three tough guys, I still wouldn't have drifted off with my tail between my legs, not having gone so far. And they were only dames!

I said: 'I'll go. But when I go, I'm gonna take somebody with me.' I stared hard at Blondie's face. 'How about telling me where you got those shoes, sister?'

Instinctively, all three of them glanced down at the white sandals Blondie was wearing. That was why I'd picked Blondie out from the others. They were all wearing black, high-heeled shoes. But Blondie was wearing white sandals. And they were a very unusual type of sandal. I ought to know, because I'd bought them. I'd bought them for Sally.

Blondie musta seen immediately what I was after. She seemed to automatically take command of the situation.

'Suzy,' she said meaningfully. 'Helga!'

It amused me the way those dames acted. It was like they were gonna attack me. They spread out in a semi-circle. Helga was over by the wall. She reached up and took down a stock-whip, a whip with a long thong and a short, stubby handle. She threw it across to Blondie, who caught it skilfully. I grinned. Wielding a stock-whip in that confined space meant she'd do as much damage to the other girls as to herself.

But Blondie had other ideas. She wound the thong around her hand. She kept winding it around her hand until the stock of the whip was dangling at the end of a short foot of thong. Then I got it. That whip, the way it was, made a pretty good sap.

I made up my mind I'd have to keep a close eye on Blondie. And it seemed I'd have to keep a close eye on the other two as well. Suzy and Helga were advancing towards me from the sides. Suzy had got a lariat in her hand. Then Blondie began to move in towards me.

There was something mighty confident and mighty unpleasant about the efficient way they were closing in. It wasn't the kinda way you'd expect dames to act.

I watched Blondie carefully. She was swinging the stock-whip menacingly. If that whip haft happened to catch me, it'd give me a lotta pain. I wasn't gonna wait there for things to happen.

I still had Helga's skirt in my hand. I'd been holding on to it automatically. I flung it suddenly straight at Blondie, straight in her face. It wrapped around her head so she couldn't see, and at the same moment, I launched myself at her. I smacked into her hard, and we both went sprawling on the floor. Instinctively, my hand reached out, grabbed her wrist and held tightly to prevent her using that whip. That was the only thing that worried me. And that shows just how much I underestimated those dames.

As soon as I hit the floor, with Blondie's soft body

squirming under me, the other two heaped themselves on top. One got her arm crooked under my neck and yanked me backwards at the same time as she pulled my hair with the other hand. The other dame began gouging for my eyes with her thumbs.

Defensively, I went in the direction I was being pulled, instead of resisting. That rolled me off Blondie and left me on the floor with the two dames clinging to me like limpets. I struggled to get free and heard Blondie say, 'Okay.'

That musta been a signal, because both girls rolled clear. I got a good view of Blondie swinging that whip. It was driving straight at my head, and all Blondie's weight was behind that swing.

Somehow I got my head outta the way. I almost didn't do it. The whip haft whistled along the side of my face, taking the skin off in parts, and thudded into my shoulder, just at the base of the neck.

The pain was agonising. I felt my shoulder tingle right down to my fingertips before my arm went suddenly numb. But even so, I was still thinking. I rolled. I rolled hard. I rolled so hard that when I hit Blondie's legs, it knocked them from under her, so that she sat down on top of me.

And then the other two dames piled in on top on me. Blondie was spread-eagled over my body, clinging on to one of my hands. Suzy had her weight across my legs, and Helga was sitting on top of my head, grappling with my other arm.

Maybe some guys mighta considered it fun, struggling with those three dames when they had the kinda curves that they did have. Especially when the total clothing the three dames were draped in, added together, wouldn't have made a respectable swim suit for a respectable girl. I seemed to be smothered in round, soft curves. If you ever get three dames piled on top of you at some time, you'll see what I mean.

But it wasn't fun. Those three dames meant business. I couldn't believe it at first, because they were just dames. But when the dame sprawled across my thighs began winding the lariat around my legs, I got it. These dames really did mean business. They were gonna truss me up.

I tried to get my hands free. But there was a dame clinging to each hand. They'd got their weight spread over me so I couldn't even roll. And Helga, sitting on my head, was nearly suffocating me.

I suddenly realised that I was nearly a goner. They had only to get my legs roped and I'd be a plaything for them to handle. If I didn't get loose from this quickly ...

I saw it differently then. They were dames, and subconsciously I'd been treating them like dames. If I was gonna get outta this, I was gonna have to forget they were dames!

I forgot they were dames! Somehow I managed to twist my head and open my mouth. And then I bit. I bit as hard as I knew how. I didn't know or care what part of Helga it was that I bit, provided I got free.

Jeezus, what a howl that girl gave. She leaped up so suddenly, she almost took my teeth with her. That left my shoulders loose so I could strain upwards and clop Blondie under the chin. Blondie hadn't been expecting that. She went rolling backwards with her long legs splaying. I wriggled quickly, twisted around and got Suzy off my legs. I scrambled to my feet and was no sooner erect than Suzy, who had managed to get a coupla turns of the lariat around my ankles, jerked me hard onto my backside again. Blondie leaped on my shoulders, got her leg crooked around my neck and put on pressure so it was like I was being strangled. At the same time, she grabbed my hair with both hands and began tearing my whole scalp loose.

Helga musta been hurt when I bit her. There was blood running from the upper part of her thigh. I just caught a glimpse of it as she swung with her high-heeled shoe. A dame's shoe is pretty light. But it's pointed, too, and with a lotta steam behind it, it can hurt. Helga put a lotta steam behind that kick. She was good and mad and she wanted to hurt. That kick landed in the pit of my belly. Not quite where she meant it to land, I guess, but it hurt. For a second or two, there was a rushing sound in my ears as agony screeched through me. And then I saw red. I got my hands around Blondie's ankle and almost twisted her foot off. She gave a screech and released her leg pressure from my neck.

I reached up, got hold of her hands as she tugged at my hair and, with a sudden jerk, pulled her right over on top of me. She landed just in time to take a second kick from Helga. I grabbed Helga's ankle, tugged and brought her down hard. That left Blondie and Helga sprawled there almost side by side. I spread my around their necks and smashed their heads together as hard as I knew how.

They were dazed, and I was nearly on my knees when Suzy brought the chair down on me. I sensed it swinging down, tucked in my head and took most of the blow on the hump of my shoulders. I twisted quickly, grabbed the chair and pulled it outta Suzy's hand. I musta looked mad because, for the first time, the dame looked scared. She even backed up from me a little.

I climbed to my feet, watching her carefully as I disentangled my legs from the lariat. She was scared. But nevertheless, she was watching for an opportunity to dash in again. Blondie pawed at my thigh. I was getting fed up by this time. This could go on all night if I let it. Blondie was on her knees, her face was tilted up towards me and her chin was sticking out invitingly. I let her have it as hard as I knew how. Her head clopped back and she sprawled on the floor without a sound.

Helga was holding her head and moaning. She didn't seem to know what was going on any more. I swung at her, too. She didn't even know what hit her.

And by this time, Suzy really did scare. She was at the door, trying to wrench it open.

I got up behind her, slipped a coil of the lariat around her white neck and jerked on it hard. She forgot about everything except trying to tear the rope from her neck so she could breathe.

I loosed up on the rope. 'It's curtains for you, unless you do what I tell you,' I said. 'You gonna play it my way?'

She nodded as well as she could. The rope was tight around her neck, and she seemed scared to take her fingers from it in case she strangled.

'Lie down on your belly,' I told her.

She went down on her knees and then, when I slackened the rope, she went right down flat on her belly. I knelt down on top of her with my knees grinding into the middle of her back. I took the rope from around her neck and tied her hands together behind her back. She must have been scared, because she didn't even wriggle. Then I slipped a coupla turns of the rope around her ankles and pulled hard on the rope until her legs were doubled back so that her ankles touched her hands. I roped her ankles and hands together.

I got up, breathing heavily. There was blood on my

cheek, and my head felt like it was gonna burst.

Suzy moaned, 'Gee, mister. You ain't gonna leave me like this? These cords are cutting me in two.'

I wasn't outta this mess yet. If these dames cut loose, it might bring all Ghost City down around my ears. I got another rope off the wall and went over to Helga. She was moaning softly, half-conscious. I propped her up against the wall in a sitting position with her knees drawn up underneath her chin. I securely lashed her wrists to her ankles. That way, she wasn't gonna do much walking. But that didn't mean she wouldn't squawk. I rolled up my handkerchief, thrust it into her mouth and tied it in place with a rope.

Suzy hadn't tried squawking yet, because she was scared what I might do. I rolled her over so she lay on her side, untied the 'kerchief from around her neck and gagged her with that. She rolled her eyes apprehensively.

Then I turned my attention to Blondie. She was still out cold, and for a moment I was scared I might have broken her neck. But when I examined her closely she seemed okay, and even moaned a little as though she was coming round.

There was plenty of rope in that place, and I made a good job of Blondie. I wasn't squeamish about it, because I was remembering how she'd tried to pulp my head with that stock-whip. I tied her hands to her ankles the same as I had with Helga, and then, for luck, put a slip-knot around her neck and ran the other end of the rope around under her thighs, tied tightly. She was okay as long as she sat with her knees up under her chin. But if she started wriggling and tried straightening out her legs, she'd choke herself.

I gagged Blondie with her own 'kerchief, stood up,

staggered over to the table, took a deep breath and swallowed a full glass of rye at one draught. I guess I needed it, and I guess I'd earned it.

I gave another look around the room. It was a shambles now. Helga's eyes flickered dazedly. First she tried to speak and then she tried to move her hands to find out what was in her mouth.

I wasn't bothering with her any longer. I went up the stairs and opened the first door. It was a bedroom, and empty. I opened the second door. And there was what I'd been looking for.

Sally was in that room.

11

When I opened the door, Sally was lying on the bed her head turned away from me and a frown of pain on her face. Her eyes were closed but I could tell she knew somebody had come into the room.

She didn't look as though she liked being there. Her outstretched arms were roped to the top bedposts, and one leg had been drawn down tightly and tied to the bottom bedpost. The leg that wasn't tied, she'd drawn as though to protect her abdomen.

And Sally hadn't got that way without a struggle, either. It musta been a tough struggle, too. They'd managed to get most of her clothes off, but she was still wearing her cami-knickers. But you'd hardly have said she was wearing them. The shoulder straps had been snapped and buttons had been ripped off. The garment was really nothing more than a crumpled piece of clothing rumpled up around her waist. Dressed or, if you like, undressed the way she was, enabled me to see just how much of a struggle she'd made.

There were long finger-nail scratches on her chest and neck, and her arms and body were blotched with yellow and blue bruises. Without opening her eyes or looking, Sally moaned, 'I won't do it. I won't do it, I tell you.'

I said softly: 'What won't you do, honey?'

That startled her. She jerked her head around and stared at me as though I was a ghost. And then relief, hope and joy flooded her eyes. 'Hank,' she breathed. 'Oh Hank, Hank, Hank!'

I did a crazy thing then. Here I was in the centre of Ghost City with the job of getting a kidnapped dame outta there and into safety. I was in a spot where I hadn't a moment to waste. But instead of being smart, I had to try and be smarter. I took a cigarette from my pocket and lit it slowly. I was enjoying myself. This was my moment and I was gonna gloat, just to pay Sally back for making me feel mean.

I blew a spiral of smoke towards the ceiling and said casually, 'How're you making out, Sally?'

'Get me outta here, Hank,' she pleaded. 'They'll kill me or something.'

I looked surprised. 'Don't you like being here?'

'Hell,' she breathed. 'You going crazy or something, Hank?'

I tried to look mystified. 'What's the matter? Don't you like being here? Isn't this what you wanted?'

Outside, some of the Westerners must have been staging one of their shows. Guns were going off and horses were galloping up and down the street, men were shouting. It was pretty deafening.

Sally got a little hysterical. 'Get me out of here,' she yelled. 'Hank, get me out of here.'

Deliberately, I flicked ash on the carpet. 'I'll go get Foster for you. He's your new boyfriend. He'll help you.'

She stared at me wild-eyed. 'Don't,' she pleaded. 'Don't let him come near me.'

'What, don't you like him no more?'

'He brought me here,' she said, almost in a whisper. 'He brought me here. This is what they've done, him and those she-devils.' Her voice sank lower. 'They going to keep me here, tied like this, without anything to drink or eat until … until …' Her voice broke off.

I knew what she meant. Foster intended to keep her roped that way. If she wanted a drink, she'd have to consent to pay for it … with her body. He'd probably keep her roped that way for some time, eking out food and water to her in the same way that she eked out her body.

Yeah, I knew what would happen. Sally would be kept there until she felt herself so cheap and so used that she couldn't bear to live outside of Ghost City. And if at any time she got really difficult, Foster probably knew a drug or two that would keep her docile. Yeah, Sally was all set to turn that place into a four-dame house instead of a three-dame house.

And as all this went through my mind, I looked at Sally and noticed the youthful curves of her body. There was a subtle difference between her and the three dames I'd roped up downstairs that I couldn't quite put my finger on. Sally and the others, broadly speaking, had the same kinda bodies, the same kinda curves and the same kinda skin. But there was a difference. I can't say what the difference was; it was more a feeling I had than anything else. Sally was youthful, clean and fresh. She was like a crisp, fresh radish, innocent and clean. The other dames didn't make me feel that way. Just to look at those other dames made me feel that all those sweet things that exist between man and woman were sullied instead of being sweet and fragrant.

And because Foster had tried to turn Sally into something that she wasn't, and because he was a man who had turned other girls like Sally into ways of life that were rotten, a great anger swelled up inside me.

And outside the pistols still banged away and men still shouted and horses still galloped. It was a very noisy town.

I fought down the rising tide of anger.

Sally pleaded, 'Get me outta here, Hank. Don't let them do this to me.'

'I'll get you outta here, honey,' I told her. I got out my pocket knife and went to the head of the bed so I could cut the rope around her wrists.

Those guns were still banging away outside. There was so much noise that I hadn't noticed the door opening behind me. The first I knew of it was when Foster said softly: 'Okay, Janson. Get your mitts up and turn around. Only drop that knife before you turn around.'

I froze. For a moment, I was on the point of starting something. But when a gun's pointing at your backbone, it's easy to be reasonable. I turned around and faced Foster. His handsome face grinned into mine. But there was no humour in that grin. It was a sadistic grin. The kinda grin a spider might make when he sees a fly entangled on his web. And right behind Foster was Blondie. There was murderous hate in her eyes as she glared at me. She was carrying the stock-whip, the lash wrapped around her hand and the heavy haft swinging on a short foot of thong.

Foster said: 'She makes a good recruit, doncher think?'

I made a subconscious movement towards him, and Foster jabbed with his gun. 'Get back,' he grunted.

I didn't say anything. But I looked at him, and my eyes said a lot. Foster grinned again. 'I'm glad you called, Janson,' he said. 'You've been trying to cause trouble. It's gonna be poetic justice to have you working with us.'

'First chance I get,' I told him, 'I'm gonna take you and this town apart.'

'Nice of you,' he chided. 'Now let me tell you what's really gonna happen, Janson. You're gonna work here in Ghost City. You're gonna do all what you're told. You're tough and you're smart. You'll be a useful acquisition to Ghost City.'

'Think so?'

'Sure,' he said. 'You'll be one of us, just one big happy family.'

'Sure,' I sneered. 'I'll like the job. Only tell me one thing. When does this wonderful metamorphosis in me take place? '

'Don't sneer,' he said. 'You'll be convinced. It only needs a skinful of dope and keeping you doped to the gills for a month or so. After that you'll be only too pleased to string along with us. You'll forget any petty ideals you've got now. There'll be only one thing on your mind. That'll be the question of how regularly you'll be able to get your ration of dope. And there'll be only one way to get your ration, Janson. You'll be able to get it only through me. And you'll do what I say before you get your ration.'

Sally gave a kinda moan. 'Why did you wait so long, Hank?' she moaned.

I knew what she meant. Why had I taken so long gloating over her instead of using the opportunity to get away? It made me feel bad, bumming things up that way.

I must have looked dangerous. Foster's face hardened as he directed the gun at me. 'I'm not worried about shooting, Janson. There's so much shooting going on in this town, one shot extra won't attract attention. You can have it which way you like, lead in the belly now or a dose of dope in the arm. It doesn't matter to me.'

I glared at him impotently.

Without taking his eyes off me, Foster said: 'All right, Fairy.'

Blondie moved alongside him. The look in her eye was vicious. There was an angry red weal around her throat where the lariat had been drawn tight. Blondie looked like she wanted to pay back for that. 'Turn around,' Foster ordered.

I looked at him steadily. 'Turn around,' he said again, and I could see his finger tightening on the trigger. There was nothing else for it. I turned around, slowly. I knew what was going to happen. Blondie was coming up behind me with that swinging haft. She was gonna swing it above her head and smash it down with all her strength. If I didn't get a fractured skull, when I woke up I'd feel fine ... until the effect of the drug wore off. And then I'd get another shot and another shot, a regular treatment of dope, until my system was flooded with the poison. And then, when I couldn't bear to be without it, they'd withhold the drug from me until I gibbered for it like a madman. Then they'd give me a tiny shot, just a little. Just enough to enable me to do what they wanted.

It wasn't a pleasant prospect for me. It wasn't a pleasant prospect for Sally, either. I'd made a mess of everything. I heard movement behind me, and all these thoughts were churning over in my mind, and I knew that the haft was gonna smash down in a second and ...

Could anyone, I wonder, stand still, knowing their head was gonna be smashed? Could anyone just stand there and take it? In the last second, I knew I couldn't. The odds against me being able to do anything were high. But I had to take my chance. I could almost hear the haft swishing down at me when I dodged to one side and spun around almost in the same movement.

I wasn't following any plan. I was just acting instinctively. The haft landed on my shoulder, numbing it to the elbow. But Blondie was off balance at having missed. More important still, she'd got between me and Foster.

I grabbed Blondie and hung on tightly as she squirmed. She was my shield. Foster couldn't fire without risk of hitting her. But Foster didn't get panicky. 'Keep still, Fairy,' he ordered crisply.

She obeyed him at once, relaxed in my arms. She'd squirmed so much that she was facing Foster. I had my arms wrapped around Blondie's body and kept my head tucked behind hers.

Foster levelled the gun carefully. 'Don't move, Fairy,' he said again, coldly and calmly.

I don't know how Blondie felt about it. It looked like Foster was gonna aim carefully and try to hit some part of me that overlapped Blondie.

Just to show him that wasn't such a good idea, I rocked Blondie from side to side. 'Don't struggle,' Foster warned her again. And then Foster took a step towards us, and then another. I could see what was in his mind. He was gonna get right up close, poke his gun-arm around Blondie and squeeze the trigger. That way, he wouldn't hit Blondie.

He was so sure he was on a good thing, he didn't

think of the obvious reply to that move. I did. It was tough on Blondie, but I was in a tough spot myself.

I waited until Foster was just a pace away and then I rushed him. I rushed him, using Blondie as a battering ram. At that close range, he hadn't got time to get his gun out of the way. Blondie and me hit Foster hard; so hard he went sprawling on the floor with the gun twisted out of his hand. But that wasn't before Blondie's body had skewered itself on the barrel of the gun.

Foster went down with Blondie on top of him. Blondie was moaning and doubled up with pain. But Foster was greased lightning. He rolled Blondie to one side and snatched for the gun. My foot got there first and sent the gun slithering out through the door. I went running after it, and then sprawled full-length on my face as Foster grabbed my ankle.

We rough-tumbled for a bit, and then Foster broke loose. This time, he actually got the gun. I was only a split-second after him and grabbed him by the wrist. Then it was a kinda all-in struggle, kneeing, kicking, punching, while all the time he tried to turn the gun on me, while I tried to twist it from his hand. We struggled around at the top of the stairs, and somehow I managed to get a lever on his wrist and jerk so that the gun flew over the banisters. When it landed downstairs, the jolt musta set it off. I heard the bullet tear into woodwork somewhere.

But there wasn't much time to think about things, mixing it with Foster the way I was. He was tough. He kneed me in the groin. I slapped a six-inch drive under his chin that snapped his neck back and sent him down the stairs. That wouldn't have been so bad, except that he took me with him. On the way down, I got my hands round his throat, but jolting on the stairs upset my hold.

We hit all the stairs, all the way down to the bottom. And when we hit bottom, Foster was on top of me. He didn't hesitate. He hung a sock on my jaw that nearly sent my head through the floorboards, and then he dived for the gun again. Foster seemed pretty intent on shoving a bullet in my guts.

I scrambled to my feet, and there was Foster, glancing around for the gun. He saw it the same time as I did, and he dived for it full-length. I had further to go than he, and I hadn't an earthly of getting a hold on it first. I ran and kicked at it and sent it spinning out through the open door into the street a fraction of a second before his fingers touched it.

Foster grabbed my swinging foot, jerked and brought me smashing down on the floorboards. As I hit the floor, he was on his feet, streaking into the street.

Somehow I scrambled to my feet and went after him. I saw him stoop and grab the pistol from the dusty road just as I reached the door. He was in the middle of the street now. He spun around and levelled the pistol. I could see his malicious eyes gleaming with triumph as he fingered the trigger and knew he couldn't miss. With a kinda numb feeling, I realised that this was it, and everything suddenly seemed to be happening much more slowly than it really did. In a matter of split seconds, lead was gonna tear into my body. My muscles automatically tensed themselves to resist the impact of the lead that was gonna tear through me. I saw Foster's finger tightening on the trigger. And then a missile plunked into his chest; a missile that quivered and stuck out like a quill. A look of surprise and pain glazed Foster's eyes, and he seemed to hang in the air. And then another missile struck him, skewed through his neck, severing the main artery so that blood pumped out over his shirt as the pistol dropped from his nerveless fingers and his knees crumpled.

I stared, unable to believe my eyes.

From the sideboards, a burly figure hurled itself at me, rolling us both inside. A voice I recognised as Victor's rumbled at me as automatically my thumbs searched for his windpipe.

'Get under cover, you damn fool.'

I rolled away from him and sat up.

'I've been looking all over for you,' he grumbled.

I said: 'Did you see what I saw just now?' I had an uneasy feeling that I was suffering from the DTs.

'What d'ya mean?' he asked.

'Foster,' I said. 'He was just killed.'

'I know,' he said. 'Lucky for you, too, otherwise it mighta been you rolling in the dust.'

'I know,' I yelled at him. 'But did you see what killed him? He got a coupla arrows fired into him!'

'Of course,' he said, as if that was the most natural thing in the world.

I stared.

12

When you think about life, it's wonderful how everything has a cause, a beginning. If you buy an ice cream in a drug store and it turns out to be bad, there's a reason for it. Maybe the shopkeeper has had it too long. Why? Because, on account of a big factory nearby closing down, custom has suddenly dropped off and goods he'd already ordered are turning bad on his hands. Why did the factory close down? Because ...

You can go on that way for ever, tracing things back, always finding a cause. Why did the man drop dead on Fifth Avenue without a mark on him? Ask the doctors who examined him. They found out the cause. A blood clot that had clogged in his heart.

Why did Foster fall dead with an arrow through his chest and another through his neck? There had to be a cause. And there was a cause. Victor told me what the cause was, and later on I got the full story from Jimmy Chark. Jimmy was looking after that end, and I was able get all the details from him that I couldn't get for myself. It happened this way.

As soon as Victor and I left Phillip and Jimmy so we could find Sally in Ghost City, Phillip and Jimmy decided they'd drive over to the reservation and see what went on.

Heaven knows how a man who'd had the beating up that Jimmy had endured could bear to get out of his chair, let alone go chasing all over the place. But that's what Jimmy did. As I said before, he probably had a streak of the Indian stoicism deeply implanted inside him.

When Jimmy and Phillip got to the reservation, the whole camp had turned out for an orgy of feasting and drinking. Jegger was there, sitting with the chief, wearing a presentation headdress. There was a huge camp fire burning and a number of painted braves were performing ceremonial dances to the frenzied beat of tom-toms.

A strict ration of hooch had been handed around, and some of the Indians were excited and frenzied. And there was Jegger, sitting in a place of honour, accepting gifts and pledging himself as a blood brother to ignorant men of whom he was taking an unfair advantage.

It was when Jimmy Chark saw this that the madness entered into him. Maybe it was the pain of his injuries that made him mad. Then again, maybe he wasn't mad. Maybe what he did then was one of the sanest things that could ever be done.

I'm not going to try to judge Jimmy. My job is just to tell what he did, and to add that what happened as a result of what he did, had to happen anyway.

Phillip showed Jimmy the utility van belonging to Jegger. It was loaded with expensive furs. A fortune, casually packed away, not even guarded. And just one of many such vanloads. And then together they crawled up to the wigwams reserved for the reservation teachers.

Phillip lifted the flap of one and they crawled

inside. There were eight huge casks of raw whisky inside. Each cask had a padlock on the tap, and outside the wigwam, one of the so-called teachers that Jegger supplied was on guard with a rifle. Jegger knew only too well the danger of allowing the Indians too much whisky.

It was then that Jimmy conceived his plan, whispered it to Phillip and engaged his support.

They crawled into one of the empty wigwams, stripped off their Eastern clothes and strapped leather loincloths around their waists. They smothered their dark hair with ashes and painted their bodies, and fixed headbands around their foreheads with a feather to give a finished effect.

After that, Phillip engaged the guard outside the whisky wigwam in conversation while Jimmy slipped up behind him and disarmed him.

The guard had the keys to the padlocks. They unlocked all the casks, took a coupla drinks themselves, for the hell of it, and then filled skin bags, which were normally used for water, with whisky.

Maybe the whisky itself began to get into Phillip and Jimmy. I doubt myself that they confined themselves to a coupla drinks as they threaded their way among the seated Indians, pouring powerful, undiluted whisky into pannikins that were meant to hold water.

They kept going like that, emptying water-skin after water-skin until nearly all the whisky had been used.

And long before they'd got near to emptying the casks, the effects of it had become obvious. There was a great deal of shouting now, war-whoops and a tendency for almost everyone to join in the dancing. The drums beat more loudly, monotonously, and somehow the rumble of the drums stirred the pulse.

Jegger didn't notice anything at first. And then, as excitement began to reach a point of tension, he became suspicious and watched carefully. He saw the Chief drink from a water pannikin and smack his lips, and Jegger's suspicions became fully aroused. He snatched the pannikin from the Chief's hand, smelled it, and then dashed it into the fire.

Then he rose to his feet and held up his hand for silence.

But Jegger made a mistake there. It was all very well to be the superior pale-face and assert himself while the Indians were sober and could remember the power of the United States Army.

But it was a very different thing to try to assert himself while the Indians were roused to blood-lust heat by the fumes of the whisky. There was no room in their leads for memory of the eternal vigilance of the White House.

For a moment, there was stupefied silence. Not awe of Jegger, but shock from the insult offered to their Chief. And then came a mad surge forward. Spears waved, whisky-maddened braves with rolling eyes leaped at Jegger with bare steel flashing in their hands.

Maybe Jegger would have ended there had it not been for Jimmy. Jimmy had by this time almost completely reverted to type. It wasn't so much the whisky with Jimmy, but the blood of his forefathers pulsing proudly with the feel of a new strength.

Jimmy got between the braves and Jegger and he began to talk. And when Jimmy talked, he had all the advantages of civilisation behind him. But he talked like an Indian and he talked to the Indians.

He talked long and loudly, with elaborate gestures

and eloquent symbolism. And while he talked, the whisky went around and the fumes rose stifling in a red mist that enveloped the minds and emotions of the Indians.

Jimmy talked of the past injustices that had been dealt to his race by the pale-face. He talked of the slaughter of the tribes, the slaughter of the buffalo and the starvation of the proud, bold Indian tribes. He whipped up a flowing tide of resentment that had been inborn again and again in the primitive people who inhabited the reservations. He did not forget that they had not changed since the eighteen-sixties, and he worked on them until they were maddened to the point of blood-lust, howling for vengeance and at a murderous pitch hostility.

It was then that Jimmy yelled for the attack on Ghost City.

Can you imagine that horde of primitive savages, whisky-sodden, bent only on vengeance, equipped still with the weapons that their forefathers had used many years before? Can you imagine them leaping onto their ponies, riding them bare-backed, with spears, bowie knives and bows and arrows for their weapons?

Can you imagine them streaming away from their camp, riding over the hills towards Ghost City, cresting the hills and seeing Ghost City nestled there in the valley, its dusty street illuminated to display the town just how it must have looked a hundred years ago?

When they swooped down on Ghost City, those Indians weren't living in the nineteen-forties any longer. They were back in the days when the Indian roamed the West freely, and the invading white man scrabbled hard to hold his ground against the red man.

When they swooped down on Ghost City with

loud war-whoops, they were on the warpath again, living the past as though it were today.

It was a bloody night, that night. It was a night that will not be forgotten for many years. But by a strange paradox, it was the primitive savage that wiped out plague spot and vice centre that only civilisation could have produced.

Most of the tourists managed to get away – at least, the sensible ones that didn't show themselves too much. The Indians were concerned only with the enemies they recognised, the pale-face of eighteen-sixty, dressed in chaps, Stetsons and rough shirts. And the Westerners fought back. Not too well, because they had no stomach for such a battle and because most of their cartridges were blank. But they fought back because they had no choice; they were hunted down and pursued.

Even Jegger didn't escape, and probably Jegger had it worse than anybody else. The civilised part of Jimmy had defended Jegger, had left Jegger behind at the camp, pinioned, awaiting … I don't know what, and I don't think Jimmy did either.

But even as the braves had reverted to type, so did their squaws. They were whisky-sodden too. They remembered the practices indulged in by squaws in the old days. And those were the days when a cowpoke would rather shoot himself than be handed to the squaws.

Jegger died that night. And he musta taken a long time to die. And there's little doubt that every second of that long dying gave him a thousand tortures.

13

I stared at Victor.

He said: 'The Indians from the reservation are on the warpath. They're attacking the town. They've started fires the other end of the town.

It was hard to believe that. My eyes must have shown it. Victor said: 'Just look for yourself. But watch your step.'

Cautiously I poked my head out of the door and looked down the street, and just at that moment half a dozen Indians came galloping along the street in a whirl of dust. As they flashed past, I could see their brown, painted bodies and the mad light in their eyes.

I pulled my head back quickly. I didn't like the look of the tomahawks some of them carried.

Victor said: 'Let's get outta here. We'll take the back way and work around to the car park.'

'Yeah. But I found Sally. She's upstairs.'

'Fine, we'll go get her.'

We walked over to the stairs. Victor caught sight of Helga and Suzy, both trussed up, unable to move a muscle but pleading eloquently with their eyes.

'I had a little trouble,' I explained as we went up

the stairs.

Victor stroked his flowing moustache and raised the inevitable eyebrow. 'Looks like you know how to handle trouble,' he commented dryly.

When we got upstairs, Blondie was still doubled up on the floor with her hand pressed to her belly. There was a dull pain in her eyes.

As I began cutting the rope around Sally's wrists, Victor whistled. 'What's this, a nudist colony?'

I said crisply, 'Have a look at Fairy. See if she's hurt bad.'

There was a wardrobe there. I opened the door and found a print dress draped over a hanger. I helped Sally climb into it. I guess it was a special kinda dress, because the front was cut so low it didn't cover more than twenty per cent of Sally's chest. But it was better than nothing.

I bent down and ripped Sally's sandals off Fairy's feet.

'All right,' I said. 'Let's get the hell outta here.'

Victor was helping Blondie to her feet. She was holding on to her side just underneath her ribs.

'Painful,' Victor said. 'But she ain't hurt bad.'

Blondie took her hands away, and there was an ugly torn blotch where the gun muzzle had jagged into her body. 'Jeezus,' she moaned, 'it hurts like blazes.'

I said, 'Look, we gotta get outta here. The Indians are on the warpath.'

I put my arm around Sally and she kinda clung to me as though I was her protector. Victor grabbed Blondie, and as we made our way downstairs he on elaborated my terse explanation that the Indians were on the warpath.

When we reached the bottom of the stairs, I looked around for Helga and Suzy. Then I swallowed. They were both gone. Well, that made it easier. It was gonna be tough getting two dames around to the car park. Four dames would have been even tougher.

We walked across to the door, and then quite suddenly three painted figures stepped inside to face us. They fanned out, staring at us stolidly. Two had long, gleaming knives, and one had a long spear. Instinctively we backed away from them.

Victor said: 'Don't make any quick moves. Those fellas don't wait to ask questions.'

The Indians stood watching us for several seconds, then the one with the spear seemed to be making a mental struggle. He dug deep down into the hidden recesses of his mind and said slowly, as if he was manufacturing the words: 'Want'um squaw. You give, then go. No kill.'

Victor said: 'He's making a proposition. If we hand over the dames we can go free.'

I felt Sally shrink, and her hands clutched at me more tightly.

'And if we don't agree?'

'You don't have to ask. They'll kill us and take the dames just the same.'

I said: 'I'll take the fella with the spear. You take the one on his right, and it's up to you two girls to handle the third man. But wait until I move first. I'm gonna try and get these fellas off their guard.'

I raised up my hand in the sign of peace. Three pairs of brown, inscrutable eyes watched me. 'Big Chief,' I said slowly, my mind alive with films I'd seen of pale-faces dealing with Indians. 'We powerful. We very powerful. We make ...'

The Indian who'd spoken cut me short with an eloquent wave of his hand.

'No talk. Go now. We not kill.'

I shrugged my shoulders. That spear point was still poised. It hadn't wavered the fraction of an inch. I didn't like taking my chance on grabbing it. But there was nothing else for it. I took a deep breath, screwed up my courage and tensed my muscles ...

A pony reined to a halt outside in a swirl of dust. A brown, painted Indian slid to the ground almost in the same movement. He called out something. The three Indians fanned to one side so that he could come in.

I musta been looking at him for several seconds before I recognised him, and then I gave a gasp of surprise. He turned and threw me a warning look. A look that said clearly, 'Don't recognise me.'

Victor caught the look. He said warningly, 'Don't say anything, Hank.'

'I won't,' I told him.

Jimmy Chark went on talking to the Indians. They talked slowly, with elaborate gestures, and at last Jimmy turned and looked at us. He spoke quickly so that the other Indians couldn't follow him: 'String along, fellas. I'll get you outta this mess somehow. But my influence is limited. If you start anything, I can't hold these fellas back. I've proposed that we take you back to the camp as hostages. If you come quiet, there won't be any trouble. And tomorrow's another day. They'll have thick heads tomorrow, the father of all hangovers and a horror of what they've done today, coupled with an unholy dread of the consequences. Will you string along, fellas?'

Victor said: 'That'll be easier than getting a knife in the belly. But are the dames safe?'

'I'm hoping so,' said Jimmy. 'That's the chance you gotta take. But there's no chance at all now if you get tough.'

Sally said: 'I'm willing to chance it.'

'Okay, let's go,' I said.

Jimmy spoke a few more words. The Indian with the spear nodded his head. Then he looked at Sally and stepped forward. Jimmy said sharply, 'Don't move. He won't hurt.'

The Indian went close to Sally. His face was expressionless as he stuck his thumb in the corner of her mouth and levered up her lip so he could see her teeth. I was seething inside. The guy was placed just right for a quick smash on the point. But Jimmy's eyes were upon me warningly, even pleadingly. I held myself in check. The dress Sally was wearing didn't hide much. The Indian pulled it to one side so that it didn't hide anything. Then he pulled up her skirt so he could see her thighs.

'Hold it, Hank,' breathed Victor.

I held it. But I was burning all over, trembling on the point of letting fly with my fist.

The Indian gave a grunt that seemed to signify satisfaction and stepped back.

'Okay, fellas, let's go,' said Jimmy.

The four of us walked out through the door, and then I saw what Jimmy was worried about. There were another dozen Indians outside. Even if we'd bettered those three Indians inside, we'd have been taken apart by those outside.

And it seemed to be quite a party, because those Indians had got Helga and Suzy. And the way they were handling those dames showed pretty clearly just what they reckoned they were going to do with them.

The Indian with the spear grunted something.

Jimmy said, 'You're to walk along the sideboards two abreast. If you try to escape, they'll kill you.'

We walked along the sideboards. The Indians grouped me and Victor and the four dames together and kept us in the middle of them.

Jimmy said: 'They'll probably bind you on ponies and take you back to their camp that way.'

Blondie gave a little cry. One of the Indians had come close to her, put his arm around her almost naked body and squeezed her very hard in a certain intimate way that was very painful. The Indians grunted warningly as I got my body between Blondie and her tormentor.

I guess Suzy and Helga had been getting a lotta that. But they were still gagged the way I'd left them, and they weren't able to scream.

I said: 'Jimmy, it ain't gonna work out the way you said. These Indians have seen these dames, they've seen these dames the best way possible to make them want them.'

'String along,' muttered Jimmy. 'We'll be able to do something; you'll see.' He sounded worried.

We'd got almost to the end of the street when three Indians galloped past. One of them sent a burning arrow smashing through the top window of a house across the road. Immediately a quick volley of rifle fire sounded. Two of the Indians hit the dust, and the third galloped on, swaying from side to side.

Then the rifles sounded again, and wood splintered around us. One of the Indians gave a grunt and sank to his knees. Jimmy yelled out something. It was as though the Indians had completely forgotten our existence. They melted into shadows, became indistinct figures that fanned out and surrounded the house. Again the rifle barked, and three arrows swished through the air towards the window.

Slinky figures reached the door of the house and smashed at it with their tomahawks. For a moment, a man's figure showed at the top window, and then he crumpled as another arrow swished into the window. But the rifle still kept sounding as it was taken up by somebody else.

'Quick, let's scram,' I said.

I got my arms around Helga and Suzy and began running with them. Victor did the same with Sally and Blondie. We dodged into the darkness of a narrow alleyway and ran as fast as we could. Behind us, the rifle was still spitting away.

We kept running, Victor leading the way. We skirted away from the town so we could circle around to the car park.

Once or twice we had to lie down in the long grass as a band of Indians galloped past.

A third of Ghost City was in flames now. Smoke swirled towards the sky and we could see the silhouettes of frenzied figures dancing around the flames. All the time, there was intermittent rifle fire, and as we got near to the car park, we came across many grim reminders of what was happening. We stumbled across two Westerners. One had a tomahawk still embedded in his back. An Indian with the back of his head blown away was still holding the haft of the tomahawk. Further on, there was a pile of dead ponies tangled together. One of the ponies whinnied with pain as we passed. It wasn't quite dead. Neither was the Westerner we found at the entrance to the car park. A sharp knife had been run around his head from forehead to back and his hair and scalp removed as neatly and as cleanly as though the Indian that did it had been in practice for years. We hurried the girls past the grisly spectacle. There was nothing we could do for him.

It seemed like most of the tourists had beaten it outta town. There were only two cars there. Needless to say, neither of them was mine. Nobody was gonna spend time picking out their own car when a band of bloodthirsty Indians was whooping somewhere in their rear.

The first car we tried was a black saloon. We just couldn't get it to start. So we went for the second car. It was about the smallest car I've ever seen. But it's engine started to life as soon as Victor tickled the starter. It was like music.

Sally got in front with Victor and I got in the back with the other three dames. Four of us in the back was just about three times as bad as the New York subway at rush hour. We nosed out of the car park and nosed head-on into a band of Indians on ponies.

'Hold everything,' said Victor. He pressed down on the throttle and leaped straight at them. For a moment they held, and then they leaped to either side. The car wing caught one pony and it squealed and reared up in the air, upsetting its rider. Another smashed his tomahawk down on top of the car as we went past.

The sharp steel bit through the roof of the car and wedged itself about half an inch above Victor's head. The Indian held on to the tomahawk. He was pulled off his mount and scuffed along, dangling alongside the car until a sudden swerve by Victor jolted him loose.

A few seconds later, a coupla arrows bounced off the back of the car, and then we were out of range.

'Keep it going, Victor,' I said. 'Get the hell outta here.'

'What d'ya think I'm doing,' he said.

I moved uneasily. I was almost buried underneath

legs and arms and all kinda curves. I remembered that
Helga and Suzy were still gagged, as well as having their
hands tied behind their backs. I got to work, untying and
ungagging. When I was through, I was sweating, and it
wasn't because it was hard work!

Helga was sprawled on top of me, and Fairy and
Suzy were pressed up tightly around me like we were
sardines. I could feel the warmth of their bodies through
my clothes, and every time I wriggled with cramp, I
couldn't help touching some part of them. I wondered if
they thought I was getting fresh.

Helga was the one I'd bitten. She hadn't forgotten
that. She said: 'You've got pretty big teeth, aincher?'

The car lurched, pressing us all over to one side.
Helga was pressed up tight against me like we were
glued together.

'Yeah, and you've got pretty big ...' I began, then
suddenly remembered that Sally was in front. She might
not have liked the kinda crack I was gonna make.

Victor drove on until we got to the outskirts of
town. Then he drew into the roadside. 'What do we
now? 'he asked.

'Drop these dames and get back to the hotel,' I
said.

Blondie grunted. 'This ain't Ghost City,' she said.

'What d'ya mean?'

'Use your head, dope. Three dames don't go into a
hotel to book a room dressed the way we are.'

That was a point. 'Where do you dames live?' I
asked.

Suzy and Helga chorused together, 'Ghost City.'

Blondie said: 'I've kept a tiny flat going over on
Palmer Street. Number two-five-three.'

Victor let in the clutch and started off again. When

we got to Palmer Street, Blondie said: 'There's a parking lot along here on the right. Drive in there.'

We drove in and pulled up. It was dark there. Victor said, 'Now what?'

'Got your key, Blondie?' I asked.

'In my pocket,' she said sarcastically.

'Okay,' I said. 'How do I get in?'

'You can't,' she said. 'The janitor's got the key, but he wouldn't let anyone in except me.'

'All right, you go.'

'Sure,' she said. 'If you'll lend me your pocket handkerchief, I'll make the front steps before somebody hollers for the cops.'

'Don't get too smart,' I said. 'You can use the frock Sally's wearing to get inside. Then you pack three dresses and some shoes, bring them back here, and the rest of you will get something to wear.'

'I'll still need your pocket handkerchief to fill out the front of that dress.'

'I guess I can spare my handkerchief,' I said.

Sally asked, 'Have I gotta take this dress off?' She didn't like it, I could tell.

'Have you any other ideas?'

Apparently she hadn't. Reluctantly she began wriggling out of the dress. It was difficult, sitting in the car the way she was. It got jammed over her shoulders. Victor said: 'Let me help.'

There was a lot more wriggling and she got the dress off. She passed it over to Blondie. Blondie wriggled around, got the door open and climbed out. She swore softly as the rough gravel dug into her bare feet. When she got the dress on, I could see she was a bigger girl than Sally. The low-cut dress didn't hide anything at all.

Sally passed the sandals over to Blondie, and then

Blondie pinned my handkerchief inside the front of the dress with a tie-pin I'd been wearing and a pin that Victor had stuck in his coat lapel. My handkerchief was just big enough to bring her almost to the point of respectability.

I noticed that Sally and Victor were sitting close to each other with their shoulders touching. I said to Helga and Suzy, 'You dames ain't got no place to go?'

'We lived in Ghost City,' Helga said again.

Sally said: 'I can go back to my hotel.'

'You can't,' I told her. 'Foster booked out for you and took your luggage.'

'Oh,' she said, and I could tell she was mulling over in her mind just how easy it would have been for her to be swallowed up in Ghost City with nobody knowing she'd been around and nobody even taking the trouble to find her.

I said: 'I've still got a room at the hotel. You can use my room.'

'What about you?'

'I'll bunk down with Victor. Okay, Victor?'

'Sure,' he said. At the same time, he slid his arm around Sally's shoulder, and she didn't seem to mind. I suddenly remembered that things could get a little hot up there in the front. The darkness was the only kinda covering that Sally was wearing,

'What about us?' asked Suzy. She'd been through a lot, the same as we all had. She sounded like she was on the point of breaking up.

I said: 'I'll tell you what. Victor, you drive Sally back to the hotel and then come back for me. I'll stop here with these girls at Blondie's place and try phoning hotels. We'll save time that way.'

'Sure. That's an idea,' said Victor. I grinned to

myself. The way things were working out up front, it seemed like Victor would appreciate having Sally's company for a while. And the reason I grinned was that I didn't mind Victor being alone with Sally a bit. In short, I'd got Sally out of my system. She was a cute kid and I liked her. I didn't like seeing her in trouble, and I wanted to get her outta trouble. But that was all there was to it now. And if she was gonna find herself a boyfriend, I'd just as soon it was Victor as anybody. He was a grand guy and I liked him a lot.

And just to clinch it, just to show the way Sally was feeling too, she didn't argue. The arrangement musta suited her fine.

Blondie got back with a suitcase. She'd brought three dresses with her. The girls struggled into the dresses, smoothed them down and thrust their bare feet into high-heeled shoes. I noticed that Victor helped Sally enthusiastically to get her dress on, and I noticed that she didn't object very strongly.

I said to Victor: 'Come right back and pick me up.'

'Okay,' he said.

'Goodnight, Sally,' I said.

She took my outstretched hand. 'Goodnight, Hank,' she said. 'And thanks for everything.' There was a kinda friendly warmth about the way she took my hand that I liked.

Then me and the three girls walked up the street towards Blondie's hang-out as Victor nosed the car towards the other end of town.

Blondie lived in an apartment house. It wasn't exactly a salubrious district. The carpet in the entrance hall and on the stairs was threadbare. As we went in, the janitor raised his eyebrows when he saw that there were four of us. But he didn't say anything. He turned his attention back to a pulp magazine.

And that showed what kinda dump the place was. It was three o'clock in the morning when this happened!

14

Blondie was exaggerating wildly when she said her flat was tiny. Minute was the word I should have used, myself. Her flat consisted of just one square room with a little cupboard attached that served as a kitchen.

When we got inside and two of them sat on the narrow divan and Helga and me sat in two not-very-large armchairs, the flat was crammed to overflowing.

Blondie said: 'Well, what do we do now?' Her face was still creased with pain, and as she spoke she unbuttoned the blouse of her dress and slipped it off her shoulders down to her waist so she could examine the ugly bruised blotch on her skin just beneath her ribs.

I got up and probed around with my finger. There weren't any ribs damaged, as far as I could tell, but the skin was broken and lots of blood vessels had been ruptured. There was no refrigerator in that flat and consequently no ice, but I made a cold-water pack and fastened it around Blondie's waist with my tie. When I was through, Blondie's face had stopped being white. It was beginning to look grey. Blondie had been on the receiving end of a lotta trouble this night, and it was beginning to tell on her.

I said: 'You look lousy.'

'I feel worse.' She put one hand to her forehead and closed her eyes like she was gonna faint.

'Better get into bed,' I advised, and pulled back the divan cover and the top sheet.

'Yeah, think I will.' With an effort, she got to her feet and wriggled so that her frock fell down around her ankles. As she stepped out of it, she said: 'Hang it up for me, willya fella? I guess my clothes are about all I got left now.'

I took her dress and hung it up behind the door. Blondie worked her legs down inside the sheets. Apparently she was content with her g-string for a nightgown.

Suzy said: 'I'm feeling whacked, Fairy. Mind if I come in with you?'

Blondie gave a grunt, half of pain and half of assent.

'Take my dress off first,' she said. 'I don't want that creased up.'

There wasn't much room on the small divan for both of them. But they were so whacked I guess they didn't mind a little discomfort. It seemed like they were asleep as soon as their heads touched the pillows.

I looked at Helga. 'How about you? If I pull these two chairs together, it'll make up a bed for you.'

'I ain't sleepy, fella,' she said. 'I'd as soon sit up for a while.'

'Okay.' I shrugged my shoulders. 'Anything you say.'

I reached for an old-fashioned telephone fixed on the wall. I dialled a coupla numbers just to see if there was hotel accommodation. I didn't get very far. It seemed like the hotels were full around that town.

'You got a cigarette? 'asked Helga.

I stuck a cigarette in her mouth and lit it for her. She looked at me with her black eyes, and there was a kinda insolent, challenging look in her eyes.

'You're gonna be awful tired in the morning,' I told her.

She shrugged her shoulders and crossed her legs. She was careless the way she did it, and if she'd been wearing underclothes I'd have seen a lot of them. 'I just don't feel tired,' she said.

The phone rang. I snatched it up quick before it disturbed Blondie and Suzy. But the way they were sleeping, I doubted if anything less than a twenty-five pounder would have awakened them.

Victor said: 'That you, Hank?'

'Yeah. Did you get Sally to the hotel okay?'

'Sure,' he said. There was a guilty note in his voice that made me smile.

'You gonna pick me up?' I asked.

'Look,' he said. 'That's what I've rung about. This car's broke down. I'm right over the other side of town from you and can't get the damn thing started.'

I thought that over.

He said: 'Grab yourself a taxi and come right over. I'll meet you at my flat.'

'I've got a better idea,' I told him. 'Morning ain't far off now. I'll stop here tonight and give you a ring in the morning.'

'Well, if that's all right with you.'

'Sure. That's okay. I've got a chair with a cushion on it. I've spent nights under conditions lots worse.'

I could sense his awkwardness right the way along the wires. He said: 'There's another thing, Hank.'

'Yeah?'

'It's about Sally.'

'Yeah? '

'I wanna get it straight. She's your dame, isn't she?'

'She's a friend of mine.'

'Just a friend ?' His voice sounded pleasantly surprised.

'We kinda had an understanding,' I told him. 'But it broke down. It wouldn't have worked out.'

His voice was excited now, like that of a kid of seventeen.

'You mean I won't be treading on your toes if ... if ...'

'She's all yours,' I reassured him. 'Sally and me are just good pals.'

'Phew,' he breathed. 'I guess I feel a lot better now I got that off my chest. I kinda couldn't help myself, and I was feeling a bit of a skunk on account of not knowing where you stood.'

'That's all right, Victor. You ain't got a thing worry about. I'll ring you in the morning.'

'Thanks a lot, Hank,' he said. 'Goodnight.'

'Hey! Just a minute.'

'Yeah?'

I said, 'Best of luck, Victor.'

'Thanks, fella.'

I put down the phone and found Helga's black eyes pondering on me. She said: 'Seems like you went to an awful lotta trouble to hand your girlfriend over to Victor.'

'I'm crazy that way. Any time I happen to see a dame being recruited for a vice squad, I don't do anything about it unless she happens to be my dame. Then I do it just so I can pass her over to my pal.'

'You got a down on Ghost City?'

'What do you think?'

She flicked ash on to the carpet. 'Ever think what mighta happened to Sally if you hadn't breezed along?'

'Sure. She'd have starved to death.'

Her black eyes pierced into mine. 'No,' she said, shaking her head. 'Dames ain't heroic, they're materialists. And life's pretty sweet, mister.'

'You oughta know. You were in the business.' I couldn't help the scorn creeping into my voice. And somehow, the scorn in my voice got home to her. Her eyes dropped. She didn't blush. She didn't have it left in her to blush. But I'd got under her skin. She took a quick drag at her cigarette and said, without looking up:

'Blondie came to Ghost City about three years ago. She came under the same circumstances as Sally. I guess she hated it much about the same as Sally hated it. She went for four whole days without water before she gave in. They kept her tied up that way for two whole months until she was earning three meals a day. And by that time, she was a different girl.'

'There weren't no chains holding her down,' I pointed out. 'She had the opportunity of scramming outta Ghost City any time.'

Helga said: 'It was different afterwards. When it's happened once or twice, I guess you feel a bit mean about yourself, maybe you hate yourself more than a lot. But when it's happened a lot, it does something to you. You feel different. You feel different from other people, and you are different from other people.'

'It takes all sorts to make a world.'

'There's lots of other things, too,' Helga went on. 'Having gone so far, Blondie had a lot to stay on for. She got food and a roof over her head. That's more than she'd get outside. If she'd left Ghost City, she'd have had maybe a bench in the park and a ticket for a Salvation Army free soup canteen.'

'She coulda got a job.'

'With no clothes to wear and no money!'

'She'd have got along.'

'Maybe,' said Helga. 'Maybe not. But if she stayed in Ghost City for five years, there'd be so much set aside for her every week, and when she left in five years' time, she'd have a nice little nest-egg to start life again with. If you can take it, it's not a bad life, and Fairy had learned to take it.'

I said: 'At the end of five years, she wouldn't have got her dough and she couldn't have left, anyway.'

'There's honour among thieves, you know. They had to get new girls all the time, and they had to play straight if they were gonna continue to operate. They played straight, too. Lots of girls left at the end of five years with their little nest-egg. It set them up. They got drug-stores for themselves, or road cafés. They even got themselves husbands, sometimes.'

'And Foster let them walk out after five years?'

Helga grinned. 'Don't be old-fashioned. Those dames had to go after five years. You been around Ghost City. They were all young dames, weren't they? The guys that ran Ghost City thought it bad policy to have dames around who even looked like they wouldn't be young much longer.'

'All right,' I said. 'You made a case for Blondie. But how comes she's so willing to get other dames into same jam as she was in. How comes she helped Foster with Sally?'

Helga asked for another cigarette. She puffed smoke across towards me. 'That's the way dames are,' she said. 'She'd been driven along that road. She didn't like to see other dames getting by. She kinda reckon that what had happened to her should happen to other dames. In some way, it made her feel better.'

'I don't get it,' I said.

'You wouldn't,' she said. 'But Suzy does. She's the same way. Any time a snooty dame takes a tumble, she gets a kinda kick out of it.'

'Suzy got converted same as you and Blondie?'

Helga puffed smoke again. 'Suzy didn't take much persuading. She'd been on the grub line for three days when Foster found her. The offer of a square meal was all she wanted.'

'How long did you hold out?' I asked.

'Me?' her eyes widened and then closed to narrow slits. I could see her black pupils flashing through the slits. 'I was a walk-over,' she said. 'I just walked right up to Foster and asked him to take me on.'

'A volunteer,' I said, just a shade bitterly.

'Yeah,' she said. 'A volunteer.' She seemed determined to flaunt the fact as though it gave her a secret pleasure.

'I guess you had your reasons,' I said softly.

'I had a reason,' she said bitterly, and there was a break in her voice. 'I had a fella. The finest fella that ever walked. When he got shot down over Germany, II guess nothing else mattered. I couldn't stop thinking about him. So I tried to make myself forget. And every time there was a man, I tried to tell myself I was forgetting.'

'And did you forget?'

'I forgot,' she said dully. 'I forgot so well that it's impossible now for me to remember him, what he was like, the way he looked at me and smiled, the touch of his hand.'

I could imagine. Sweet memories trampled into

insensitivity by the coarse and lustful desires of many men.

'What are you going to do now?' I asked.

Her black eyes glittered. 'What are any of us going to do? We lost our jobs, remember. We lost our homes, too. We ain't even got a set of clothes to stand up in.'

'Yeah.' I thought that over. Blotting out Ghost City might be a good thing for the community as a whole. But it was tough on the folks that had to get their living outta Ghost City. These three dames were an example of what the end of Ghost City was gonna mean to some folks. These three dames were skinned, even down to their clothes, and it was sure gonna be difficult getting themselves a job with Ghost City recorded as their previous employment. The only dames employed in Ghost City were on the vice end of the town.

I put a call through to Police Headquarters. I reported my car had been lifted from Ghost City. The cop there said:

'Don't worry too much about your car, fella. There's too many guys wondering about their scalps.'

'How bad is it over there now?'

'Kinda easing down. They just about burnt Ghost City down. There ain't no point in sending the fire brigade. That old timber burns like matchwood.'

'That's the end of Ghost City, eh?'

'Just about. Them Injuns musta been crazy to bust out that way. Looks like we got another Injun War on our hands.'

'It's that big?'

'Nuts,' he said. 'I was just ribbing. Most of them are high-tailing back to the reservation. Somebody musta smuggled hooch into the reservation and gave them an overdose.'

'Well,' I said. 'If someone hands in my car, send it over to my hotel, will you?' I gave him my address.

'Okay, fella.'

When I nestled the telephone back on the receiver, Helga had gone to sleep. A lighted cigarette still dangled from her fingers. I reached out and took the cigarette from her and stubbed it in an ashtray that had been an advertisement handout for a tyre manufacturing company.

Dawn wasn't far off now. But even a cat-nap might be a good idea if I wanted to live through the next day. I took off my jacket and draped it over Helga, eased my aching feet out of the hot leather and tried to get comfortable. It wasn't easy to get comfortable, but I went to sleep just the same. I guess I musta had a tough day, too, like all the others.

15

It was the telephone that awoke me. It kept digging down at me as I slept. I tried to brush it away, tried to shut my ears to it, and then suddenly I was fully awake and the phone was ringing like it would never stop.

I got the phone off the hook and heard Victor's voice at the other end.

'It's eleven o'clock,' he said. 'You still sleeping? '

I yawned loudly.

'I'm over at your hotel,' he said. 'Your car's been handed in. A fella and his dame grabbed it last night. The cops told them to turn it in to the hotel.'

'That's right,' I said. 'What's new?'

'Ghost City's washed up,' he said, almost smacking his lips with satisfaction. 'The Injuns have gone back to the reservation and Ghost City is in ashes.'

'What's the toll? 'I asked.

'Fourteen Ghost City fellas are cold, five will need new sets of hair and about thirty are being treated for various injuries. That's according to the Oke Monitor.'

'Not so bad as it coulda been,' I said. 'How did the Indians make out?'

'That's not known. They took their dead and

wounded back with them. They've got all the county cops over at the reservation now trying to sort out what happened. They gotta kinda iron curtain down. Reporters ain't allowed within a mile of the reservation.'

'It coulda been a lot worse,' I said.

'Sure it could.' He paused. 'How about coming over for lunch?'

'Where?'

'At the hotel, here. I'm gonna ask Sally to come.'

'If you're sure you want a threesome …?'

'Sure I'm sure.'

'Okay. See you about one.'

'That's a date.'

I hung up, stretched my face with a yawn that reamed out the creases of my skin, and wandered over to the cupboard that was the kitchen.

I filled the sink full of water and plunged my head in it. I felt a lot better when I'd finished drying my hair on the tea-cloth. There was a cracked mirror, which I used to comb my hair. While I was combing, Helga, who must been half-wakened by the telephone, got up and stretched herself. Then she crowded in the cupboard with me and got a coffee-saucepan stoked up.

'Anything to eat?' she asked.

'Help yourself.'

She dug around, found a bagful of eggs and some Ryvita bread. 'Scrambled?' she asked.

'Suits me.'

I squirmed my way outta the cupboard and found a hinged flap screwed to the wall. When it was propped up, it was about big enough to hold four cups.

Helga poured the coffee and then wakened the other two. In the early morning light, with their make-up smeared and their hair all over their heads, they looked pretty blowsy.

I went over to the window and opened it wide. The window overlooked a dirty back-alley where folks shoved out their garbage cans to be collected. It was littered with rusty tins and bits of paper. Two or three mangy cats scratched at rubbish piles.

There'd been four of us crammed into that tiny room all night. The window had been jammed tight all the time. Maybe that was the reason that when I opened the window over that filthy back-alley, the air that came in seemed fresh and sweet and life-giving.

Blondie and Suzy sat up side by side and sipped their coffee. Blondie's face looked lined with worry now. Helga slapped a yellow mess on a plate and handed it to me with a fork. I ate with the plate balanced on my lap.

Blondie said: 'Any news from Ghost City?'

'Yeah. It's burnt out. Nothing left.'

She gave a bitter kinda smile. 'That's fine and dandy,' she said.

I shoved a forkful of scrambled egg in my mouth and chewed it some. Then I waved the fork admonishingly at Blondie. 'Why don't you three dames get smart?' I said. 'Why don't you give over this easy kinda living and try earning dough the hard way?'

'What do we do now, sing psalms?'

'I'm not riding you,' I said. 'I'm trying to help.'

Blondie threw back the coverlets, got outta bed and strode over to a cupboard door. She opened it. Inside were a few bits and pieces of clothing hung on hooks.

'Take a good look, fella,' she said. 'That's all I've got in the world. Not even the cups and saucers in this flat belong to me.'

Helga said, 'I haven't even got that much.'

'You'll get through,' I said.

'Just how?' asked Blondie.

'Something will turn up,' I said vaguely.

I stopped offering advice after that and concentrated on eating. I wasn't responsible for Ghost City being burnt down. But in a way I felt guilty about those three dames. Maybe it was none of my business and none of my responsibility. But that didn't alter the fact that these three dames were in a jam.

I pushed away my plate, sat back and lit a cigarette. The three dames took it in turns to wash. Then they got out what bits of clothes Blondie had and began trying them on. It seemed like Blondie's wardrobe consisted of three dresses, two brassieres, two very flimsy pairs of pants, and a few pairs of stockings, mostly darned. That wasn't a helluva lot of clothes to share between three. Somebody had to go short somewhere.

They didn't seem to mind me being there, so I just sat back and watched. Maybe if things had been different, I mighta got hot under the collar, seeing all that femininity on show. But I couldn't get it outta my mind that those three dames came from Ghost City. Maybe it was true they hadn't wanted it in the first place. But … it made it different somehow.

Helga eased a flimsy pair of lace panties over her hips and then swore softly as the button came off. Suzy was having trouble adjusting straps on a brassiere that had been set for Blondie. Blondie was sitting on the bed easing transparent stockings over her long legs.

I said: 'Would you dames take a chance to live differently if you got a chance?'

Blondie looked at me suspiciously: 'What kinda chance?'

I shrugged my shoulders. 'I dunno. Maybe a job or

something.'

Helga said: 'You aiming to be a good Samaritan or something?'

'Take it that I'm crazy,' I said. 'Just what do you dames expect of me?'

Helga looked at Blondie, and Suzy looked at both of them. Helga moistened her lips with the tip of her red tongue and said: 'Maybe it's too much. But we'd like some dough to grubstake us for a coupla days. Say about twenny bucks.'

I grinned.

Helga kinda froze. 'Okay,' she said. 'We didn't ask for money.'

'Keep your hair tucked back,' I said. 'I had another laugh coming to me. What a ride Foster took you dames for. A hundred bucks a time they wanted from fellas down there, and you three dames need just twenny buck to stake you for a coupla days.'

'Why don't you read us a section from the Bible?' sneered Suzy.

'Whatsay you take a powder?' Blondie suggested.

'Okay,' I said. I got up, put on my jacket slowly and fastened my tie. I dug down in my inside pocket and got out my wallet. I hadn't been carrying much dough around with me and I needed taxi fare back to the hotel. I had about sixty bucks to spare. I put it on the table. Blondie said: 'What's that for?'

'That's for three dames in a jam,' I said.

'Look, mister,' she said. 'We don't want that kinda money. We've been getting dirty cracks outta you all the time. We don't want sermons and we don't want sermon money. We heard you; you don't have to pay us to listen.'

I said seriously: 'Look, I wanna help. You're in a

jam. I don't care what you do with that money. Use it the way you want. There's no strings attached.'

She looked like she still wasn't gonna take it. Then somehow she musta felt my sincerity. 'Okay, mister,' she said. 'It'll help, and we're grateful.'

I got back to my hotel and went up to my room. Sally was making up her face. She went on making up her face while I washed and shaved and climbed into another suit that didn't look like I'd been sleeping in it all night. There was just about time then to go downstairs for lunch.

Victor was waiting for us, washed, fresh and clean, with his moustache well combed and flourishing, a carnation in his buttonhole and a fresh piece of sticking plaster on his cheek.

We had cocktails and then drifted over to the table. As we ate, we talked of Ghost City. Then I told them about the jam the three dames were in.

Victor said: 'Look, I'd like to whack in a coupla Cs.'

'How's your pocket-book?' I asked.

'Okay, right now. I got paid up by the broadcasting company.'

'All right,' I said. 'Hand over.'

Sally said: 'I guess Ghost City kinda cleaned me out, too.'

'Yeah?' I said. 'What happened to that dough you won on the wheel?'

'Tucked away in my suitcase,' she said.

'Looks like the dames got a raw deal outta Ghost City,' I commented.

'Not so raw for Sally,' said Victor. He looked at Sally meaningfully. She smiled back at him and took his hand under the tablecloth.

'What goes on? 'I asked.

Victor looked sheepish. 'We kinda got talking on the way back to the hotel,' he said.

'Yeah,' I encouraged. 'Don't be shy. I'm a man of the world.'

He wasn't sure what I meant, but he cleaned up any doubt. 'There's nothing that grandma wouldn't approve of,' he said. 'But me and Sally found that we sorta … well … you know.'

'You tell me, Sally,' I said. 'For the first time I've known Victor, he's at a loss for words, so it must be something extra special.'

'It is extra special,' she said, and her eyes were shining with a kinda happiness you don't see in folks' eyes these days. 'We're going to be married.'

'What!' I almost yelled.

'Sure,' said Victor.

'But … but …' I spluttered.

'That's the way we wanna do it,' said Victor. 'No waiting, no hanging about, no uncertainty. We're gonna do it right away.'

'Is that how you feel too, Sally?'

She nodded her head, thoroughly sure of herself.

I sat back in my chair. 'That calls for a double brandy,' I said.

They had it all worked out. They were starting for Lone Springs immediately, where a twenty-four hours' residence was sufficient to obtain a legal marriage.

'You ain't upset, are you?' asked Victor.

'Upset! I'm delighted. But I'm surprised outta my life, too.'

Victor leaned across the table confidingly. 'I'll tell you something. I'm surprised outta my life, too.'

They were so set on getting hitched as soon as possible, they went right off immediately after lunch. I stood on the steps and watched them until they were out of sight.

Then I went back to my room and packed. It seemed to me like I'd had a bellyful of Oklahoma City. If I stayed here till I was a hundred and two, it was unlikely I'd see as much action in that time as I'd seen in the last three days.

I had all my stuff loaded into my car, drew some dough from the bank and settled my bill. Then I started off driving outta town.

I was thinking of the route I was gonna take and was almost outta town when I remembered about the two hundred bucks Victor had given me for the dames. I turned around and went back.

When I pushed open the door of Blondie's flat, they were still there. Helga was hanging on the end of the phone and the other two were sitting staring at her moodily.

'Hello,' I said. 'Interrupting you?'

'Want your dough back?' asked Blondie.

I put the two C-notes on the table. 'Contribution from a friend of mine for three dames in a jam,' I said.

Helga started speaking then. She said, down the mouthpiece, 'What the hell does it matter where I worked before? Do I have to have a pedigree before I can iron sheets?'

She listened for a few moments and then said a very rude word into the telephone before she jammed the receiver back on its hook.

'We're gonna be crucified,' she said.

'Who were you talking to?' I asked.

'What's it to you?'

'Just curious,' I said.

'You can tell him,' said Blondie. 'Let him gloat.'

'Yeah, have a gloat,' said Helga. 'Three reformed girls trying to get a job. Having a good time. That's the third agency, and there's nothing doing unless there are testimonials forthcoming.'

'That's interesting,' I said.

Suzy said, 'It's a groove. It's worn too deep. We ain't gonna be able to buck outta the groove. We're floosies and we've gotta stop that way.'

'Maybe you'd stand another chance in another town?' I suggested. 'Some place where they've never heard of Ghost City.'

'Transport costs dough,' said Helga. 'So does a hotel, and grub while you're looking for a job.'

I was gonna say something crazy. I knew it, but I couldn't stop myself. It's just the way I am, I guess.

I said: 'I've got a proposition. I've got a car outside and I've got enough dough to grubstake you three dames. I'll take you along with me. When we hit a town, you can find a job. If you get one, okay, I'll stake you for a week or two. If you don't, I'll carry on to the next town.'

All three stared at me. 'What kind of a gag you pulling?' Blondie demanded.

'No gag at all,' I said. 'I just happen to be the kinda guy that does these things. I got enough dough, too, so we can get by.'

'I believe you mean it,' said Helga.

'It's not so much if I mean it as much as if you mean it … about getting a job, I mean.'

Suzy said challengingly, 'I've got nothing to lose. I'll take you up on it.'

'It goes for all three of you,' I said.

Blondie looked at Helga. There was a query in her eyebrows.

'Let's take him up on it, just for the hell of the thing,' said Helga. She looked at me, and her dark eyes flashed challengingly.

'You dames got much to pack?' I asked.

'We're wearing it all,' said Blondie.

'Okay, what are we waiting for?'

I could tell they weren't sure if I was ribbing them, but when we got downstairs and they saw my car, I could see they were impressed. I chased away a coupla urchins who were scrambling on the running board, and showed them how I packed my stuff away so I could camp any time I wanted.

Then they climbed inside and bounced up and down on the cushions.

'Gee,' said Suzy. 'This is real comfy.'

'Well,' I asked. 'Are you coming along like I suggested, or are you gonna stay here?'

Suzy said: 'I'm going along, mister.'

Blondie said: 'I'm beginning to think you ain't such a bad guy, even if you do preach.'

Helga said simply, 'Can I ride alongside you?'

We got outta town and hit the main drag for the next State. It was a beautiful afternoon, the sun was shining and the trees looked green and refreshing after being in town. I pressed my foot down on the throttle and felt the powerful engine respond, hurtling us along the road noiselessly.

I glanced in my driving mirror at Suzy and Blondie. The gentle, soft swaying movement had been like a lullaby. They were both asleep.

I reached in my pocket for a cigarette, but before I could find the package, a cigarette was placed between my lips. I shot a sideways glance at Helga. She was occupied with lighting a match. But as she held the flame to my cigarette, her eyes looked into mine. I looked back at the road. As she put her arm down, she brushed my arm.

'Tired?' I asked.

'A little.'

'We don't hit a big town yet-awhile,' I said. 'How would you three dames like to camp tonight? Get some real fresh air into your lungs instead of city smells.'

'Suits me fine.'

I could feel the touch of her arm against mine, and I moved over a fraction so that the pressure of her arm against mine was stronger. She pressed back.

'Like to go to sleep?' I asked.

This time, when I shot a sideways glance at her, I caught her smiling at me with wicked black eyes.

'Could I?' she asked.

I reached out and put my arm around her shoulders. She kinda twisted around and nestled in the crook of my arm, so that her head rested on my shoulder. Somehow she seemed small and pathetic and in need of protection.

'Comfortable?' I asked.

'Uh-huh.'

I kept my arm around her, with her head nestling against my shoulder. Long after she'd gone to sleep, I kept driving, driving straight into the sun with the tyres eating up the road and carrying me on and on towards I knew not where.

ALSO AVAILABLE FROM TELOS PUBLISHING

CRIME

THE LONG, BIG KISS GOODBYE
by SCOTT MONTGOMERY
Hardboiled thrills as Jack Sharp gets involved with a
dame called Kitty.

MIKE RIPLEY

Titles in Mike Ripley's acclaimed 'Angel' series of comic
crime novels.

JUST ANOTHER ANGEL by MIKE RIPLEY
ANGEL TOUCH by MIKE RIPLEY
ANGEL HUNT by MIKE RIPLEY
ANGEL ON THE INSIDE by MIKE RIPLEY
ANGEL CONFIDENTIAL by MIKE RIPLEY
ANGEL CITY by MIKE RIPLEY
ANGELS IN ARMS by MIKE RIPLEY
FAMILY OF ANGELS by MIKE RIPLEY
BOOTLEGGED ANGEL by MIKE RIPLEY
THAT ANGEL LOOK by MIKE RIPLEY

HANK JANSON

Classic pulp crime thrillers from the 1940s and 1950s.

TORMENT by HANK JANSON

WOMEN HATE TILL DEATH by HANK JANSON
SOME LOOK BETTER DEAD by HANK JANSON
SKIRTS BRING ME SORROW by HANK JANSON
WHEN DAMES GET TOUGH by HANK JANSON
ACCUSED by HANK JANSON
KILLER by HANK JANSON
FRAILS CAN BE SO TOUGH by HANK JANSON
BROADS DON'T SCARE EASY by HANK JANSON
KILL HER IF YOU CAN by HANK JANSON
LILIES FOR MY LOVELY by HANK JANSON
BLONDE ON THE SPOT by HANK JANSON
THIS WOMAN IS DEATH by HANK JANSON
THE LADY HAS A SCAR by HANK JANSON

NON-FICTION

THE TRIALS OF HANK JANSON
by STEVE HOLLAND

TELOS PUBLISHING
Email: orders@telos.co.uk
Web: www.telos.co.uk

To order copies of any Telos books, please visit our
website where there are full details of all titles and
facilities for worldwide credit card online ordering, as
well as occasional special offers.

Printed in Great Britain
by Amazon.co.uk, Ltd.,
Marston Gate.